THE
Twin Kingdom
SERIES

MORE THAN WHAT THEY SEEMED

PANEQUE Y DIAZ

outskirts
press

Outskirts Press, Inc.
http://www.outskirtspress.com

Paperback ISBN: 978-1-9772-4200-6
Hardback ISBN: 978-1-9772-4253-2

Library of Congress Control Number: 2021908695

Cover Photo © 2021 www.gettyimages.com. All rights reserved - used with permission.

Outskirts Press and the "OP" logo are trademarks belonging to Outskirts Press, Inc.

PRINTED IN THE UNITED STATES OF AMERICA

To my loving and supportive family.
The bravest and strongest group of men and women in the world.

"Hacia atrás ni para ganar impulso!"

MAGJID

CHAPTER ONE

The Kingdom of Sonastare, 1845

The rumors did not do her justice. She was beautiful, gracious, and gave every appearance of being open-minded as much as open-hearted. With his experience and proven track record, this should not take much time at all. Would that all his targets were as shiny and vulnerable.

Enough work for tonight. He needed a drink and some mindless conversation with the idle members of the upper crust. Crossing the crowded ballroom, he kept a steady pace toward the main entrance and his waiting coach. He'd make first contact this week.

Lady Analisa Hastings, Dowager Marchioness of Walsenburg was enjoying her evening out immensely. There was nothing particularly unique about this night or this event. Like every other ball during the season, all the beautiful members of the Elite were garbed in their finest, preening and posing for all to see. The agendas were as varied as the gowns, with marriage-minded young ladies and their eager, desperate mamas looking to capture a titled heart or at the very least an influential eye. This was more the opportunistic papa's objective.

There were finely dressed gentlemen focused on making lucrative business connections with others looking for a brandy-weakened moment to close a deal. Some were simply enjoying an evening out, happy to be in such close proximity to the top echelon of society in the kingdom of Sonastare, one of the smaller world kingdoms but certainly one of the wealthiest. Understated and very old noble blood held together a realm steeped in social structure and advantageous alliances.

The social Elite or the top 1 percent was made up of centuries-old families dating back so far, their history was more legend than confirmed fact. This was of little consequence since the Elite's money, power, and influence dictated truth in Sonastare. There was, of course, a royal family. Contrary to most royals of the age, this exceptionally elusive clan preferred anonymity to notoriety. Although they very clearly governed Sonastare with an iron grip, very few knew who they were or could identify a family member at twenty paces. No portraits of the family hung in the museum or in public buildings. An invitation to the Fortalesa Palace was rare and seldom without a specific and essential purpose. Few ever revealed the intent of a palace visit but everyone anxiously prayed for the invitation regardless of the circumstance.

There were two annual social events held on royal grounds. The kingdom's anniversary ball, held each June, commemorated the coronation of Grand Duke Juangelo Morejón as Sonastare's first unanimously crowned ruler at the defeat of Prince Sebastian in the Garrix Wars. This sixth and final battle severed the economic ties binding the people of Sonastare to the now extinct principality of Leonell. Since then, the grand duchy grew and prospered into the thriving kingdom we know as Sonastare. All credit was given to the Morejón family through generations of progressive and visionary leadership.

The second event was Las Mirabellas. This was the most elegant and extravagant social event in the kingdom. Most would claim it was the social event of the continent if not the world. No expense was spared. Every detail was at an exalted level. The occasion achieved several important goals; it provided rare accessibility to the royal family, it showed the world Sonastare was wealthy and in control, and it offered a medium for sharing upcoming changes to the kingdom directly from the monarchy. Not simply modifications in governance but pending nuptials and births among other things.

Since the death of her husband two years prior, Analisa felt blessed to be associated with a less ambitious strata in this dazzling display of wealth, power, and beauty. As a widow, she enjoyed a certain level of independence rarely found but zealously relished by those fortunate enough to secure it. The vast majority of lovely ladies surrounding her this evening had only one subject on their minds: gossip.

"Ana, it is lovely to have you back in our circle. We have missed you these past two years." Margarete Bellins, Viscountess Cross and Analisa's lifelong friend, bubbled with enthusiasm.

"My dear! I must admit, I am enjoying myself immensely." Analisa reached out to cover Maggie's hand with her own. "I feel ever so light and carefree. And with you here, I feel as if we have traveled back in time to when we were both young girls sharing secrets."

At three and forty, Analisa was certainly not old. She knew she would eventually look toward a future with hopes of love and passion. But for the present, she was happy to enjoy the simple pleasures and freedom of widowhood.

"I understand Her Grace is planning to have this season's Mask the talk of the Elite for years to come." Margarete asked optimistically, "You will be attending, will you not?"

"I would not miss it. Ada has promised to come help me select the perfect costume for the event." Analisa looked around the ballroom with an approving eye. "There are so many new faces this season. I look forward to making friends with each and every one of them by the time the Marlan Gala comes around."

"Shall we take a turn around the ballroom? I have a few new friends you simply must meet," Maggie suggested with an uncertain smile. She would be crushed if Analisa refused to accompany her. They excused themselves from their small group and began to slowly make their way around the large and elaborately decorated main ballroom.

Three bands played in concert, overlapping yet beautifully harmonizing and blending their lovely melodies as the dancers seemed to float effortlessly around the magnificent pink marble salon. Hundreds of candles illuminated every inch of space highlighting the fire in every diamond, sapphire, and ruby present. The smiles were as brilliant as the jewels with hopes and rumors of soon-to-be nuptials. This is where fairy tales were born.

Thomas Smyth crossed the receiving room at Folton's. Not exactly White's of London but a top-class establishment catering to the upper crust of Sonastare's society. Membership was expensive but not as exclusive as White's. A common man with a common name easily blended in. Provided he also had deep pockets. As long as you talked a good game and treated your companions to the occasional round of quality drink, no one questioned your lineage or your motives.

Thomas Smyth wasn't his real name of course. It was simply his current alias and the most important tool of his unorthodox trade. Since he was a small boy, he knew his greatest strength was in inspiring the trust of those in his orbit. Regardless of education, social standing, gender, position, or vocation, he could easily bring those around him into what he called "The Mist," his world. It wasn't always what he genuinely believed or what society considered right or wrong. This he left to the philosophers and legal minds. Thomas enjoyed creating new realities for himself and seeing how long it would take to bring others into this same truth. At two and ten, he had convinced the children of three neighboring properties, having a bridge shared by all three estates, that the bridge was equally the domain of all three families. He had enjoyed working them into quite a frenzy over a few weeks' time, ultimately convincing them he should be allowed to manage traffic on the bridge, for a small fee of course. He had collected several coins before his father was made wise to his scheme and ended his career as the local troll.

Thomas wasn't too disappointed. His goal was not the accumulation of wealth but the power he felt he wielded over others. That was all it took. From that point on, he moved from scheme to scheme, and game to game. Only now, the games were more elaborate, often involving vast sums of money and numerous players. For this reason, he was much more meticulous in his preparations and executions.

For the past several months, Thomas had been researching every detail of Lady Analisa Hastings' life. The dowager marchioness had just made her reappearance into society after two years in mourning for Darston Hastings, fifth Marquess of Walsenburg. From all indications, the marriage was one of affection and mutual respect. The marquess was six and ten years the lady's senior, with the marriage being arranged by the families for mutual benefits. They had two children: George Hastings, the sixth and current Marquess of Walsenburg, newly married without issues, and Evelyn Maddahs, Countess of Trenton, married one month prior.

The dowager marchioness and her husband had lost a son to hemophilia before he was eight, a loss that still saddened the lady from time to time.

Both her ladyship's parents, the Duke and Duchess of Colton, were deceased, leaving no direct heir to assume the Sonastare Duchy. Although Analisa, as a female, could not inherit the title or its entailed estates, which would be inherited by her cousin, all property and possessions owned by her parents yet not entailed to the title were bequeathed to Lady Walsenburg upon their deaths, a mere six months after the loss of her husband. The unentailed assets were vast and complex. There were currently so many solicitors, officials, and governments involved, there was still no clear or accurate accounting of what Lady Analisa Hastings was actually or accurately worth. At least this information was not yet common knowledge. Thomas Smyth had connections. Both legitimate and otherwise. Although he was still gathering data, he knew more than most and he knew what that meant. Our beautiful widow was a significant target and a literal treasure to whomever found themselves in control of all that Lady Analisa did not yet know she possessed.

The day after the first ball of the season greeted a mild, sunny morning. Analisa rose at a quarter past eleven, as a maid brought in her morning-day meal. She was accustomed to rising early each day while in mourning, but last night had been her first back in the whirl, and she had vowed to enjoy every blessed moment.

She lay still in her enormous four-poster bed as the maid set her meal at the table by the window overlooking her meticulously manicured gardens. The dower house wasn't huge, but it was elegant, modern, and very well appointed. She and Darston may not have been in love but they did come to love and respect each other greatly. He took very good care of her while by her side and made sure she would be well taken care of after his passing.

Listening to the maid hum a soft, soothing tune while busy at her labor, Analisa replayed last evening in her mind. She had met so many lovely people. The young had so much energy and so many hopes and dreams for the future, one could not help but be washed away in their exuberance. It was so sad her son would not allow himself to share in that joy. He and his wife, the newly minted Marquess and Marchioness of Walsenburg, were present. He looked so annoyed. It made Analisa feel sad for him. He was always a serious boy and didn't routinely make wise decisions, but he was a titled noble with wealth, health, youth, and property. Why not enjoy the blessings the Lord gives you?

Evelyn was still on her honeymoon and would return within the next few weeks. Analisa and her daughter didn't share similar personalities and had always had a strained relationship. Her daughter wasn't comfortable with demonstrative displays of affection, and Analisa loved to show her children a great deal of open affection in private and whenever possible. *Oh well*, she thought, *maybe the next generation will want my uninhibited hugs and kisses.*

With a wide smile she greeted the morning and her servant with an enthusiastic "Good morning, my dear."

The maid came over, drawing the bed curtains, ready to help her mistress rise. "Good morning, my lady. Did you sleep well?" Georgette had been with Analisa for the past six years. She could not think of working for anyone else. When Lady Walsenburg retired to the dower house, Georgette enthusiastically accepted her ladyship's request she join her there.

"It was a wonderful night, awake and asleep, Georgette." Analisa smiled, rose, and went to break her fast as she wrapped her robe tightly around her. "How is the world this fine morning? Please tell me something good."

"It is a lovely, sunny day, my lady. The weather is mild and perfect for relaxing in the gardens." Georgette knew how much Analisa loved spending time outside. "Shall I call for Tully to help you dress?"

"That would be lovely, Georgette. Please ask her to come in after my meal. I will be wearing the new blue day dress this morning, dear, if you will let Tully know."

The maid smiled and bobbed a curtsy before departing to attend to her mistress's wishes.

CHAPTER TWO

Thomas had been up for hours. When planning for a campaign of this magnitude, one could never be too careful or study the facts too often. He'd gathered a few additional tidbits last night while sharing brandy and stories with his social acquaintances. The new Marquess of Walsenburg was not well liked. He was reputed to be self-indulgent and living well beyond his means. He was not a bad person from what could be gathered from his half-drunken mates. It simply was that there were no positive qualities to recommend young Walsenburg. He was poor at management and leadership, lacked social skills, and could not choose a good investment if given a single option. He was friends with the Count of Trenton, his new brother-in-law. It appeared both men shared poor character qualities. What Thomas could not know was the depth of devotion the dowager marchioness shared with her children. The urgency of his campaign would largely depend on this variable. He would need to do more digging to accurately ascertain how far from financial ruin the two lords were before they would turn to her ladyship for assistance.

He'd put Teddy on the hunt. The boy was a ferret when it came to uncovering the deepest and darkest. He wrote a quick note requesting Teddy meet him at the Lamb's End for an update this evening and dispatched the note with a trusted local runner. Thomas didn't think it would take long to uncover the information he needed. The lords were young and very new to their titles. Although Thomas assumed they'd had very little time to accumulate any significant debts, he knew that a downward spiral could take these men into ruin quickly. No need to think the worst. *Let's gather the facts and move forward from there.*

This evening was the Cartingtine Musicale. He had confirmed the dowager marchioness would be in attendance. Although he could not secure a legitimate invitation, getting into these events was not very difficult. Thomas possessed two of the most important and obvious weapons in the art of deception: he was uniquely attractive and disarmingly charming.

His mother was from India and had been a breathtaking beauty her entire life. Her dark skin and large, light brown doe eyes drew the attention of everyone who crossed her path. Her melodic voice would almost mesmerize her audience whether she was singing or simply sharing a story.

His father was of European ancestry and commanded attention and respect even at his most relaxed. He was well over six feet tall with a lean, muscular build, moving with more grace than any man had a right to possess. His parents had met quite innocently on one of his father's trips to India. It was absolute love at first sight for them both.

Thomas was their third child and the light of his mother's life. She would always say that Thomas was the best she and her husband had to give. He had inherited her dark skin and captivating eyes. The sharp and pronounced features of a god with hair so deeply black, strangers felt compelled to reach out and touch it without realizing they were doing so. From his sire, Thomas had received his impressive height, gracefulness, and commanding presence.

He had never felt the sting of rejection. Wherever he went, he was welcomed with open arms and showered with bottomless affection and attention. What made Thomas even more dangerous was what was inside the splendid packaging. Thomas was highly intelligent as well as being humorous and empathetic. He knew he could not lose. And never would.

"Good evening, sir. May I have your name?" A very imperious look-ing man in gold and black livery stopped him at the door.

"Good evening. I am Mr. Thomas Smyth and a guest of Lord and Lady Tarquent." Thomas knew the Tarquents would be here this eve-ning and had a bad habit of inviting friends along to these types of events. It would not be questioned even if the retainer had the time and ability to follow up on the story. "I was not given a formal in-vitation as Lady Tarquent promised to speak with Lady Cartingtine personally."

The footman gave Thomas a thorough assessment but decided it was not worth the trouble to turn him away. There would be approxi-mately two hundred guests this evening and one more didn't signify. Moreover, the man certainly dressed and carried himself as a member of the Elite. "Certainly, Mr. Smyth. I will announce you."

Thomas slowly descended the main staircase while carefully tak-ing inventory of the assemblage. As part of his research, he not only gathered background on his target but on the environment and its occupants.

He quickly recognized a few faces with whom he'd socialized on previous occasions. These would help cement his character and le-gitimacy in society. They would also help him make the important introductions with those who possessed the power and influence he required to further entrench himself in the roll. He needed to be known but, most importantly, he needed to be trusted.

Spotting two men he recognized deep in conversation at the back of what would soon be the musicale's stage, he moved slowly through the crowd, making it a point to greet as many guests as possible. He always approached them as if they had met before and shared a secret. No one wanted to admit they were missing something, so everyone played along. The key was to keep the encounter brief.

Eventually he made it to where the two men stood. "Malcolm, I did not know you were attending this evening." Mr. Malcolm Gillam, second son of a wealthy Sonastarian merchant. His father expected him to serve as his eldest brother's second-in-command when he inherited the family shipping business. Malcolm was not happy but he was compliant. They'd met at Folton's the previous evening along with his friend Mr. Barns Braiard. Barns was of little value but a connection nonetheless. And a wealthy one at that.

"Thomas, I was not aware you were acquainted with Lord and Lady Cartingtine." He didn't look as if he really expected an explanation, so Thomas didn't volunteer one.

"I was not sure I would be attending. Fortunately, my previous plans changed unexpectedly and here I am." He looked around as if disinterested in the overall attendance. He was actively looking for the dowager Lady Walsenburg. He needed to gain an introduction to the lady this evening. "Quite a crush this evening. I have attended many a musicale in my day, but none as well attended as this one promises to be."

"It is not the musicale per se that draws the crowd, my friend, it is the circumstance. This is an important venue to see and be seen. Particularly for the marriage-minded members amongst us." Barns elaborated with a sinister smile. "There is greater opportunity for conversation with a lady you may be interested in courting than you would find at a ball. Are you looking for a bride, Smyth?"

"I cannot say I am looking for a bride, but I am not opposed to keeping my options open." Thomas again surveyed the room with apparent new interest. "My preferences run to a more mature woman.

Independent and no-nonsense. Elegance, beauty, and grace are a must." Thomas thought he did a fairly good job of describing Lady Walsenburg. "Anyone in attendance fit that description?"

"Sounds as if our Thomas here is looking for a widow to warm his bed." Both men laughed. "Are you shopping for a wife or a mistress?" Barns winked and smiled.

"That would largely depend on the lady herself, would you not say?" Thomas hoped the conversation wasn't so crude that it would eliminate Lady Walsenburg from consideration.

"Well, if it is a warm and lively bedmate you desire, Lady Gilgood has my full recommendation. She is energetic, creative, and very adventurous. She is also discreet, since she is still technically in mourning for her not so dearly departed husband." Just then Malcolm looked to the top of the staircase and smiled widely. "However, if you are interested in quality, there is only one lady that comes to mind."

Thomas turned to look in the direction Malcolm was still smiling. There, at the entrance landing stood his prime objective. Draped in blue satin that looked to have been fashioned for the queen herself stood the dowager Marchioness of Walsenburg.

"That is top-shelf, quality goods right there, my friend. It is rumored Lady Walsenburg is sinfully wealthy. Her bloodline extends so far back, scribes are still sorting branches on that family tree."

Impressive assessment. It seemed the lady was held in high esteem by most. At least by the few with whom Thomas had spoken. This adventure was proving to be more rewarding than anticipated. "How can I secure an introduction to the lovely lady?" Thomas looked hopefully at the two men, who kept their gaze on Lady Walsenburg. "Gentlemen?" The two broke out of their trance.

"I wish I could help you, Thomas, but I am afraid I am not acquainted with the lady." Barns looked sincerely apologetic.

"I cannot help either, old man. We have never been introduced." Malcolm looked around. "My aunt Marie may be able to gain you an introduction if you have your heart set on it." He looked toward his left, where an older woman was having an animated conversation with a younger lady. "Aunt Marie knows everyone. Or at the very least, knows someone who knows everyone." He motioned toward where the lady stood. "Come along. I will introduce you and see if we can get the ball rolling."

The men approached quietly. "Pardon me, Aunt Marie." Malcolm gently touched the elder lady's elbow. "I would like to introduce you to a new friend. Aunt Marie, may I present Thomas Smyth of Scotland."

"A pleasure, my lady." He gave an elegant bow.

"Mr. Smyth, I present to you Lady Marie Grossman, Baroness Kelt."

"The pleasure is mine, Mr. Smyth." She gave Thomas her hand and a genuine smile. "You are certainly one of the handsomest gentlemen I have had the pleasure of meeting this season."

Thomas bowed again and kissed the air just above her gloved hand. "You flatter me, my lady. If my looks please you, I have only my dear parents to thank. I will pass along your compliment when next I see them."

Lady Kelt immediately tucked her hand in the crook of Thomas's right arm. "Tell me, my exotic boy, are you married?"

Thomas could hear the wheels turning in Lady Kelt's head and heart. He'd bet a quarter of his ill-gotten gains this lady was already making a list of potential Mrs. Smyths for him to meet.

"I am not yet married, my lady, nor am I actively in the market for a better half at the moment. However, if the fates deem I meet the future mother of my children in the near future, I would not run for cover." This further sparked the lady's interest. No doubt about it, she was making plans.

"Well, you simply must allow me to introduce you to some of our more eligible young ladies while you are here with us. I know every lady of quality in the kingdom." She gave him a confident smile. "I would like to have you over to my home for tea soon. Will you come?"

"I would be delighted, my lady." He was about to broach the subject of Lady Walsenburg when Lady Kelt was distracted by a new guest.

"Would you excuse me, gentlemen? I see Lady Roselane has just arrived. I must speak with her before the performance commences." She turned to Malcolm. "I will see you before we leave, yes?"

"Of course, Aunt Marie." Both Thomas and Malcolm bowed as Lady Kelt departed.

There was no guarantee Lady Kelt could be his conduit to Lady Walsenburg but it definitely showed promise. After all, if she didn't know the lady herself, she would know who did.

Analisa stood for a moment on the mezzanine, taking in the scene. Her face lit up with joy as she recognized so many of the attendees. Several ladies demurely waved in her direction when she caught their eye upon her introduction. Etiquette dictated she was not to show too much emotion under any circumstances. She had been instructed her entire life on how a lady behaves in public and in private, and Lady Walsenburg was the epitome of elegance. The challenge was that Lady Analisa Elizabeth Childress was one of the most genuinely emotional people the good Lord had ever placed on earth. She felt, and what she felt, she showed or was tempted to show, if not for her strict, disciplined upbringing. In her mind, she had never been able or even desired to suppress her emotions. The best she could do was to manage them. At least in public. In private, that was a different matter, as her children and her dearest friends could attest to. She even credited the success of her marriage to the fact that she genuinely loved Darston Hastings, and had always let him know just how much. Although he was more reserved in his affections, she knew he reveled in her devotion and regard for him.

Analisa slowly descended to the main salon with all the elegance of an empress. She made her way to the refreshment table more as a place to go, rather than out of hunger or thirst. Maggie would be here this evening but she had yet to locate her.

"Ana, my dear" came a familiar voice from her right. Ada Robelight, Duchess of Welby, approached, her arms outstretched toward Analisa in greeting. When she reached Ana, she kissed her lightly on both cheeks and took both her hands in hers. "How wonderful to see you here this evening. I have been telling everyone you would be attending but I was not sure until I saw you descending the staircase. You look absolutely exquisite."

"Flattery will get you anything, my dear." They both laughed. "But do you not think it a bit self-serving to flatter me on a gown you helped me select yourself? Not very well done of you at all, dearest."

"Oh pish. A gown is only as beautiful as the lady wearing it makes it." They linked arms and walked toward the theater. "I believe Maggie is running a little bit late, but I have no doubt she will be here before the musicale begins. For the moment, I want to reacquaint you with a few old friends you have not seen in almost two years." She stopped as if struck suddenly by what she'd said. "Did I say 'old'? What I intended to say was 'long term.'" They both giggled like young girls caught gossiping. "Let us get started. So many people to see and so little time."

"The Marquess and Marchioness of Walsenburg." The arrival of Analisa's son and daughter-in-law was almost on cue. Few turned to acknowledge their arrival.

"Did we really have to make an appearance?" George Hastings, the sixth Marquess of Walsenburg, grumbled to his wife as they descended the main staircase. "I detest these events."

"George, please behave yourself. We have few friends as it is, and we have a position to uphold." His wife Joseline squeezed his arm.

"Your parents were the most prestigious nobles in Sonastare when they held the title. I do not want our reign to diminish their accomplishments or place a shadow on our descendants' future."

The new Marquess and Marchioness of Walsenburg were struggling in every respect. Although George had inherited the Marquisate with all its lands and riches, he had very little knowledge of how to properly manage his inheritance. George had always been resentful of his parents. As a child he believed that as a noble in the top echelon of a thriving and extremely wealthy and influential kingdom, it was their right and responsibility to keep the appropriate distance from those he was taught by his tutors were below his station. Smiling and calling retainers by their names was beneath them in George's opinion. Only those with titles equal or greater than his own were worthy of his time and attention. Which is why he felt it insulting to have to mingle with those of lower ranks at events such as these.

To further worsen an already bad situation, George did not feel he should give any time, attention, or credence to those in his employ, regarding the management and operation of his estates or business interests. He often made decisions in opposition to those he considered inferior, simply to demonstrate his authority over them and what was his.

When discussing business and investment opportunities with other nobles and businessmen, His Lordship made it clear to anyone not equal in rank that their advice was merely another minor variable in his decision-making process. More often than not, he went against their recommendations. He inspired no loyalty from his staff and garnered even less respect. As a result, his estates were in tatters and his coffers were hemorrhaging funds.

The former Joseline Mason—now Hastings—was the eldest daughter of the Duke and Duchess of Dials, a small and impoverished duchy on the border of the kingdoms of Sonastare and Artemisia, a neighboring kingdom to the east. Joseline and George's marriage had been arranged. Mostly by George himself. As the son and heir to a wealthy Marquisate, George felt he had an obligation to marry equal to or above his station or not at all. Due to his lack of social skills, he did not have many options. In his twentieth year he felt obligated to select a wife, and found Joseline Mason his only viable option. Though the daughter of a duke with an impressive ancestry, Joseline's family had very little to recommend them. Numerous conflicts over the centuries had rendered the duchy of Dials almost destitute. The duchy being so close to the border of two powerful kingdoms meant divided allegiances and often costly devotion to two masters. No wealth or influence meant no choice for young Joseline. When approached by the future Marquess of Walsenburg, the Duke of Dials didn't hesitate. He blessed the match without reservations or conditions.

The Marquess and Marchioness of Walsenburg tried to talk their son into delaying his decision. He had several years before he ascended to the title and several more to find and choose a wife. George was adamant. It was Joseline and no other. Six months later, George and Joseline became Lord and Lady Hastings in a mediocre ceremony heralding a mediocre life.

"Good evening, Lady Kelt. I hope I am not intruding." Lady Kelt turned from her conversation with her sister, directing her attention toward Thomas.

"My dear boy. You are not intruding in the slightest." She turned back to her sister. "Mariana, this is the young man I was telling you about. Is he not exquisite?"

"Quite a handsome youth indeed. I am Mrs. Mariana Jacobson." She extended her hand. "What can we do for you, young sir?"

Thomas bowed over both their hands. "If it is not too much of an imposition, I was hoping for an introduction to the dowager

Marchioness of Walsenburg." He looked confidently at both ladies. "I have been hearing extraordinary things and wish to make her acquaintance. Would either of you be kind enough to do the honors?"

Both ladies looked at each other with some amusement and surprise. "The introduction is a simple matter, my boy. Lady Walsenburg is a dear lady with the kindest heart you could imagine. I would counsel you to caution. She is just out of mourning for her husband and her parents. She is in a delicate state and we will not have her hurt."

Thomas put on his most disarming grin. "I assure you, my ladies, I wish only to make her acquaintance."

"Come along." Marie stood and linked her arm with Thomas'. "She will enjoy meeting you, I think. She loves people and hearing about faraway lands and dashing adventures. Besides, being surrounded by women at all times does get tedious. Would you not agree?" A baiting comment if ever he'd heard one. Several responses came immediately to mind, but not appropriate enough for his present company. Thomas simply gave her his most innocent smile with a slight bow as they laid in a course in the direction of the dowager Marchioness of Walsenburg.

Analisa had just finished her story and was turning around when she first saw him. The initial impact took her by surprise. He wasn't handsome. This man walking toward her was what she would consider beautiful. His hair was pitch black with dramatic waves over slightly longer than fashionably worn. His eyes were large and brilliant. She would swear you'd be able to see every detail from across a crowded room. He was tall with broad shoulders and slender hips. There was confidence and strength in his walk. His features were delicate but at the same time extremely masculine. But what made her heart thunder was that smile.

"Ana, you look radiant, my dear," Lady Kelt greeted as she approached. "Have you had any word from Evelyn?" She looked to Thomas. "Lady Walsenburg's daughter was recently married. It was a love match. Is that not wonderful?"

"My little girl is a married woman now. I could not be happier. And I am eager for grandchildren to spoil. But not too soon, mind you."

"My lady, may I present Mr. Thomas Smyth most recently of Scotland." Lady Kelt smiled and turned to Thomas. "Mr. Smyth, the dowager Marchioness of Walsenburg."

"A pleasure, my lady." Thomas smiled brilliantly and bowed over Analisa's hand. "I hope you are enjoying the evening."

"Most thoroughly, Mr. Smyth." Analisa took the opportunity to closely and carefully assess the magnetic Mr. Smyth as best she could. He was as attractive at second sight as he was at first. There was also something hidden. Something beneath the public façade. Something sinister, dangerous, exciting. "How are you enjoying our fair kingdom? It must be quite a change from Scotland."

"It is at that, my lady, but a very pleasant change, I must admit. Everyone I have met has been so welcoming." Innocent, simple, and straightforward. First contact achieved. It could not have gone much better. "I hope you will forgive my forwardness. When I told my cousin, Mrs. Brown, I would be visiting Salassio, she asked I convey her affection if I had the opportunity of an introduction."

"How kind of you both; please share my regard with Mrs. Brown when you next see her. Will she be joining you in our fair city? I would welcome you both for tea." Analisa could not remember Mrs. Brown, but in her station, she was exposed to so many people, it was impossible to remember everyone.

"Unfortunately, she will not be joining me while I am here. She and her husband are expecting their third child, and traveling is too much of a strain for her at the moment. However, she will be very pleased we have met, and touched by your regard." He looked around the circle of ladies and knew his time was up. "I will bid you a good evening, my lady." He turned with a smile and a bow to no one in particular. "Ladies." With Lady Kelt at his side, Thomas retreated. There was, of course, no Mrs. Brown. He'd made it up as an innocuous excuse for the introduction. Everyone had a Mrs. Brown in their lives somewhere, didn't they?

Leaving Lady Kelt with her sister and bidding them good night, Thomas made his escape.

"Your mother has certainly not missed a step." Joseline both resented and admired Analisa in equal measure. The dowager marchioness had such an ease about her. She had the ability to charm and befriend an emperor as effortlessly as she would the butcher. Not that Her Ladyship even knew what a butcher was.

Why must I always go down this dark path in my mind? Joseline thought to herself. *She has been nothing but supportive since the day we met.*

"This is her world, my dear. She may not own it, but she does an admirable job of managing it and its occupants." Was that funny? George shrugged as he watched his mother hold court with the most feared and prestigious set of matrons at the ball.

"Lord and Lady Walsenburg, what a pleasant surprise," Reardon Tenison bellowed a bit too loudly for polite company as he approached. "I was just telling Sands you and your lovely lady would not be making an appearance this evening." He looked Joseline over as if she were a doxy for sale. "I am grateful he did not accept the wager. I would have lost a pretty penny."

"Abernathy." George's level of discomfort escalated as did Joseline's. She squeezed his arm. "My dear. This is Reardon Tenison, Viscount Abernathy." He turned a condescending stare toward his companion. "Abernathy, may I present my wife, the Lady Joseline, Marchioness of Walsenburg."

Reardon bowed, never taking his eyes off the nervous lady. "I hope you do not object if I steal your husband away for a moment, my lady. We have some business to discuss of some urgency."

As much as Joseline hated navigating these social waters alone, she was more uncomfortable being a moment longer in the presence of this reprobate. "Of course, my lord. I see a few of my friends by the terrace." She glanced from George to the viscount. "Please take your time, my dear." With a tentative curtsy she departed.

"What now, Abernathy? I have little time and even less patience for your nonsense this evening."

"Nonsense?!" The viscount gave an amused expression that didn't quite reach his eyes. "You have twelve days to settle your accounts with me, Walsenburg." He waited for a reaction. Any reaction. "I do not give credit or extensions, and I certainly will not accept excuses." Still nothing. "Does your beautiful wife know the forfeiture consequences? Rumor has it you are nowhere near capable of settling your debts. Is your extraordinary mother aware of what this will cost her person-ally?" Was that a flinch? Yes, it was barely noticeable, but it was defi-nitely there. "My lord." He mockingly bowed. "I hope you enjoy your evening. It looks like a storm is fast approaching." Laughing, he turned and left, bumping George's shoulder as he moved.

George was exasperated. What in the world made him venture out this evening? This was not what he had expected when he and Joseline entered the grand ballroom. A little lighthearted conversation with nobles he didn't much like, but whose support he needed. But to be upstaged by his mother, and then threatened by a lesser noble amongst the Elite. It was intolerable.

Regardless, one thing was brought crashing home. He needed to find a solution to his dilemma within twelve days, or his family name and his and Joseline's social standing would be ruined. Not to mention the burdens he had placed upon his mother without her knowledge. This was not good. And he had only himself to blame.

CHAPTER THREE

It was still early enough that the Lamb's End was not filled to capacity. Thomas quickly spotted Teddy sitting alone in a corner. He made his way across the room as if he was as comfortable there as in his own home.

"Teddy," he greeted, taking his young companion by surprise.

"Thomas. You are on time as usual." He waved toward the empty chair opposite him at the table. "Can I interest you in a pint?"

Thomas waved over a nearby tavern wench. "Two pints of whatever you have." She smiled as if expecting further requests off the obvious extended menu. He gave her a detailed head-to-toe assessment and, with his best lascivious grin, gave her a pat on the rump and sent her on her way, turning his full attention on Teddy. "What did you uncover?"

"Pretty much as we expected. Lords Walsenburg and Trenton have made several investments in shipping with a venture organization of dubious reputation. They are being promised a high return on their significant investment, but the risk is extremely high. It appears they trusted their man of business to function as intermediary, not wanting to get their hands dirty. A man by the name of Daniel Crossings. From what I have been told, Crossings has no loyalties to

Walsenburg or Trenton. Walsenburg overlooked him for a promotion when he assumed the title and Crossings has never forgotten it. He is setting the lords up for a fall." Teddy gave Thomas a moment to absorb the information before continuing. "The ships are said to be overdue, needing an additional influx of capital to make their final voyage to Sonastare's port. Walsenburg reached out to Reardon Tenison, Viscount Abernathy, for the funds. I have not been able to find out the exact amount. I do know the loan is due within a fortnight."

"What are the terms of the loan?" Thomas looked worried. Two weeks was not much time.

"I am still working on finding out that information as well. But you ought to know, Tenison is a nasty piece of work. He only deals in big money and demands significant returns on his investments. He is well connected in the darkest circles in more than just Sonastare." Teddy shook his head, never taking his eyes off Thomas. "This does not look good. If you are going to act, you have very little time to do so."

"The other variable is whether or not he has tied the dowager Marchioness of Walsenburg to this scheme." He needed to know more. "What of Trenton?"

"He is, for all intents and purposes, destitute. What funds he inherited when he assumed the title are gone. Worst of all, I do not believe his wife or his mother-in-law are aware of any of it. Walsenburg may not know either."

"Two weeks. That does not give us much time." Thomas rose as the barmaid approached with their drinks. Were her breasts that much on display a moment ago? It didn't matter. He tossed several coins on the table as he leaned in close to her ear. "In advance. I will collect next time." He looked pointedly at Teddy. "Keep digging. We need to know more." He turned and left.

CHAPTER FOUR

Thomas decided to walk the two miles to the docks. From there he would take the ferry to Bellstrand. Baroness Kelt had sent him an invitation to tea for this afternoon and he didn't want to be late. She was turning out to be a kind and supportive ally in his campaign.

At the docks he made his way to the Bellstrand anchorage and gave his name to the liveried chief steward. No one was allowed on the island without an invitation or expressed permission from a resident or the crown. This was the local residence of the 1 percent. They demanded, paid for, and expected privacy and exclusivity while in residence. It was a privilege and a responsibility to be a member of the Elite. The crown provided and the Elite accepted the privileges knowing they, too, had a responsibility to their kingdom and its monarchy.

Having cleared him as a guest of Lady Kelt's, the chief steward directed Thomas to *The Starling*, moored at dock three, one of six identical ferries exclusively designed and dedicated to transporting passengers to and from Bellstrand. The two lower decks were for transporting large items including coaches and horses. There was a crew assigned to making sure everything transported safely and any animals traveling across felt safe and were as well cared for as their human owners up above. The back of the second level was designed for baggage and trunks, with adjacent space holding the daily supplies for the ship's use and for the comfort of its valuable passengers.

Thomas was escorted to the main floor, a spacious interior cabin capable of seating one hundred and fifty passengers in luxurious opulence. There were single sitting spaces for those traveling alone or simply seeking privacy of thought. There were group and family galleries where even on a ship, there was privacy to be enjoyed. All of the furniture was uniquely designed and of the highest quality, giving consideration to its environment in durability and comfort. Once Thomas was seated, a liveried footman presented him with a refreshing cup of cold water. Thomas refused any additional refreshments but was instructed to ring the small bell on the table if there was anything further he required.

There were only a few other passengers on board as they departed for Bellstrand. All appeared to be island residents returning home from a day in town. A middle-aged couple shared an early tea with their children while directly across from them a well-dressed gentleman was having a civilized but animated argument with a colleague. It seemed that even on a short voyage as this, no time was wasted. Life was not to be interrupted, not in Sonastare.

The ferry docked at the Bellstrand port with barely a whisper. All passengers disembarked at a relaxed pace. Businessmen had their mounts waiting for them when they reached land, and several coaches stood at the ready destined for the various mansions on the island.

Lady Kelt had sent a coach to pick Thomas up at the docks. He'd considered bringing his own mount for the trip, but Lady Kelt had assured him it was only a few minutes' ride from the dock, and his horse would be unnecessary.

Recognizing the Kelt crest, Thomas headed in the direction of the distinguished coachman standing sentry by the open carriage door.

"Good day to you, sir." The coachman bowed to Thomas in greeting. "Lady Kelt hopes you had a pleasant crossing. If you will." He gestured for Thomas to board. The spacious coach's interior was as impressive as its exterior, with modern upholstery on the walls and ceiling in the same color scheme as the livery the coachman wore. The squabs were of the finest and softest leather on the market today. This world was a complete departure from the everyday.

The lady had not exaggerated. It was barely ten minutes from the dock when the coach drew to a halt in the courtyard of one of the most luxurious homes on the island. Not that it was saying much. Every home on the island was as impressive as the last and equally as impressive as the next. It was as if there was a standard of luxury to be upheld but not exceeded.

The door opened and the step lowered. Thomas alighted, stopping a moment when he reached the ground to get his bearings. The fresh scent of lavender greeted him as the main doors opened wide, allowing Thomas a view into the home at the top of the marble steps.

"Good afternoon, Mr. Smyth." A severe-looking middle-aged man greeted him with refined condescension. "Won't you come in. You are expected, sir. Her Ladyship is with the other guests in the main parlor. Would you follow me please?"

Matisse, Courbet, Monet were all prominently on display in the foyer and entry hall. The floors were all done in Italian marble as were the walls and main banisters. The butler escorted Thomas down the corridor at a purposely slower pace. This was by design, allowing a guest to fully appreciate the aesthetic beauty of the home as well as the affluence of its master.

As they entered the main parlor, Thomas took the moment just before he was officially introduced to take in not only the room, but its occupants. There were six ladies and two gentlemen besides himself in attendance. He recognized Mrs. Mariana Jacobson, Lady Kelt's sister, and her nephew Malcolm Gillam. Although he remembered having seen the other guests at previous events, he had never had the pleasure of a formal introduction. However, there was one face he had not been expecting but was very grateful to see. If anyone saw his immediate reaction in seeing the dowager marchioness, they would have thought themselves mistaken. But of no matter. Thomas was an expert at schooling his reactions to fit the circumstances and his needs. Besides, no one knew he was there.

"Mr. Thomas Smyth, my lady," the butler announced, bowed, and elegantly withdrew.

Lady Kelt immediately rose to greet him. "My dear Mr. Smyth. I am so delighted you agreed to accept my invitation to tea. It is always a gamble whether or not a single gentleman will actually show up to something as mundane as tea with a group of gossipy matrons." She extended both her hands over which Thomas gave a low bow and a light, barely noticeable squeeze. Although he was moved by Lady Kelt's candor and genuine warm welcome, there was residual joy in his reaction at seeing Lady Walsenburg. Well, there was no mystery there. He was simply happy his plan was coming together so perfectly, that was all. Her presence here meant he'd have another more intimate opportunity at endearing himself to her.

Lady Kelt turned toward the group. "My friends. This is Mr. Thomas Smyth, most recently of Scotland. The moment I met him I knew he would be an excellent addition to our little circle. Traveling the world as he does, I am certain he has no end of exciting tales to share with us." She squeezed his arm affectionately as a mother might do, saying, *I'm teasing, but be a good boy and go along with it.* "I know you have met a few of my guests, but allow me to introduce you to those with whom you may not yet be acquainted. You know Lady Walsenburg of course."

Thomas bowed to the lady. "I have had the honor of an introduction to Her Ladyship at the Cartingtine Musicale. Good evening, my lady." Analisa acknowledged his greeting with a graceful nod and a smile.

"You are also acquainted with my sister Mrs. Jacobson and my nephew Malcolm Gillam."

"Yes, of course, good day Mrs. Jacobson, Mr. Gillam." Malcolm seemed amused over the entire situation, but they'd talk later, Thomas was certain.

Lady Kelt stood a bit taller. "Now for those you have yet to meet formally." They went around and one by one Thomas was introduced to each guest by rank as was appropriate. A viscountess, a baroness, even a duchess. The last individual to be introduced was Mr. Ryan DelCroft.

"Mr. Thomas Smyth, I would like to introduce you to Mr. Ryan DelCroft. Mr. DelCroft is our foremost authority in the world of art." She turned to the other gentleman with an affectionate smile. "Ryan, may I present my new young friend and world traveler, Mr. Thomas Smyth."

"A pleasure, Mr. DelCroft. I was admiring Lady Kelt's collection as I entered. Am I wrong to assume your guidance had some influence in her choices?"

Mr. DelCroft was, for a moment, taken aback. It was considered in poor taste to discuss evidence of wealth so candidly. You were expected to enjoy the beauty around you without concerns as to how it got there or of its value. Thomas Smyth was stepping on social mores. Very daring. "Sonastare has one of the most impressive collections of art in the world, Mr. Smyth. Canvas to sculpture, agriculture to theater; our kingdom is a veritable museum in and of itself. I would challenge anyone to enter a home on Bellstrand and not be overwhelmed by the beauty of its surrounding and the exceptional taste of its proprietor."

"I look forward to it, sir. I have no doubt I will depart Sonastare much enriched for my experience."

"Now then, shall I ring for tea?" Lady Kelt stepped away, joining her sister for a moment before giving instructions for tea to be served. As everyone lightly mingled in preparation for the formal service, Thomas took the opportunity to navigate his way toward the dowager marchioness seated alone on the elegant settee by the garden windows.

"My lady. May I join you?"

"Certainly, Mr. Smyth." Analisa waved to the space beside her on the settee. "How have you been enjoying your stay in Salassio?"

"Your city is extraordinary, I must admit. As much of the world as I have had the privilege of knowing, I have yet to come across anything to equal the beauty and splendor of Sonastare."

"How kind of you, sir. I have not traveled as extensively as you have, but the few visits I have made outside of our kingdom, though extraordinary in their own way, have only managed to increase my appreciation for our kingdom and our king."

At that moment, the butler entered to introduce their most recent arrivals. "The Marquess and Marchioness of Walsenburg."

Analisa looked so very sad as she cast a glance at her son and his wife.

"Are you well, my lady? You look a bit flushed. Is there anything I can get for you?"

"You are very kind, Mr. Smyth." She recovered quickly. "I am fine really. I have only ventured back into society and am still acclimating myself to the rhythm of things."

The conversation settled back into the mundane and casual. Tea was served along with a variety of tasty biscuits and exotic pastries. Over the next half of an hour, there were a few changes in conversation partners. Through careful maneuvering, Thomas found himself seated next to the dowager marchioness once more. She had just been speaking with her son and his wife, and from the looks of things, the subject had been unpleasant for all concerned.

"If you will forgive my forwardness, my lady, you look more concerned than fatigued. I realize we have only just met, but I have been told I am a good listener and I will protect your privacy to the death." He paused to gauge her comfort level before proceeding. She seemed distracted and vulnerable. Time to press his advantage. He stood, extended his hand, and in a casual voice meant for everyone to hear, "My lady, I have been told Lady Kelt's gardens are a sight to behold. Would you do me the honor of joining me for a turn around the grounds?"

Analisa needed some fresh air. At the very least, she needed some distance to gather her thoughts. "I would be delighted, Mr. Smyth." She rose and joined him and they exited the parlor through the garden doors.

"It is a beautiful garden. So many exotic plants and flowers. There are several I would not be able to identify." He bent down to capture a blossom in the palm of his hand. "What is this one called?"

Analisa was distracted. "He was always so sadly driven. Even as a child he looked forward to his next year as the one where his life would begin." Thomas looked up at her. She wasn't looking at him but off into the afternoon sky. Was she speaking to him or simply thinking out loud? Should he respond and break the spell or... "I am sorry to burden you, Mr. Smyth, but you did offer a friendly shoulder, did you not?"

"I did at that. My offer and my shoulder remain at your service, my lady." He stood slowly, taking care not to overwhelm or frighten her. With great care and patience, he walked her toward the closest stone bench directly under a life-size sculpture of a beautiful Venus. A Brancusi, if he wasn't mistaken. They sat side by side for what seemed like minutes in complete silence. He was in no hurry nor did he expect her to elaborate or share her concerns. He was grateful for the bonding experience. He knew that a shared moment of trust was more powerful and binding than a thousand superficial words.

She looked purposefully into his eyes. "We should not be alone together for such an extended period of time, much less share personal intimacies. We have recently been introduced." She was stating the obvious simply to satisfy a societal standard which she was perfectly willing to sacrifice. She needed to talk to someone objective, and he gave her the impression of someone worth trusting. "I assume you know I am a widow just out of mourning. To add to my sadness, I lost both my parents in a tragic carriage accident six months after the death of my husband."

"My condolences, my lady. I know the pain of loss does not conform to the calendar." She was silent. "Our fashions go from black to gray, but our hearts remain shrouded in darkness until they are good and ready to find release."

"You are quite wise considering your youth, Mr. Smyth. Please forgive me. My intention was to compliment, not to sound cynical."

"No need for an apology, my lady. I am flattered you feel comfortable enough in my company to speak candidly. Please go on."

"It is not the pain of loss that plagues me this day. I had a wonderful upbringing with loving and devoted parents. I lacked for nothing and had more opportunities than most. My husband was a brilliant man, devoted and generous, who always treated me with respect and deep affection." Standing, she paced the walk as a way to spend some of the anxious energy building up inside her. "I have accepted their passing as an inevitable part of life. I am very grateful for the time we shared." She came back, sitting beside him. "Tell me, Mr. Smyth, what does it take for a man to be happy in life?"

"Any man, or are you thinking of one man in particular?" Thomas must have missed that sharp turn from grief to philosophy, but he'd go along. "As a general rule, we like to have our bellies full, our possessions intact, and our purses flush."

Her laugh caught him by surprise. It was melodious, hearty, and genuine. She didn't bother with the usual restraints noblewomen felt obligated to display in similar circumstances. She simply laughed because she felt like laughing. Thomas worried he was liking this uncommon lady more than he should. He'd have to tread lightly least emotion sabotage his well-laid plan.

"That was the pithiest, most politely censored response I have heard to date." She laughed again. "And where does female companionship fit into the grand scheme of things, Mr. Smyth? Surely a man needs a woman to make him genuinely happy, does he not?"

"That, my dear lady, would depend on the woman…and the man."

"A point well taken." The look on her face told Thomas she had begun to trust him. "You have met my son have you not?"

"We have been introduced, my lady, but I am afraid our relationship does not extend beyond the polite greeting."

"To put it candidly, Mr. Smyth, my children are my present concern. Their happiness, or lack thereof, are my current misery. My husband and I did our best to shower them with affection and support. They had the best education. They were afforded every luxury to the point of excess, and yet, they have always seemed unhappy."

"I have always thought of things like happiness and satisfaction as things an individual must find and choose for themselves. It cannot be given or taken. It is not defined by a single standard or by any one individual. The choice, as with the control, rests within each of us." He wasn't sure he was getting his point across. "I have known the poorest of men find joy and satisfaction in a simple meal with his children. I have also known those who possessed the world, and yet found no joy in living. I do not know what portion of our lives is predestined and what is left to our discretion, but whether or not we are happy or sad? Yes, my lady, I do believe that is a choice we make for ourselves."

"I thought only the clergy had the power of absolution. Are you attempting to tell me my children's unhappiness is not my fault?"

"A more accurate assessment would be how you can feel that your children's happiness was ever your responsibility in the first place?"

"Ana?" Mariana Jacobson appeared on the path accompanied by her son Malcom. "My dear. We were beginning to worry. You did not lose your way, did you? Marie's gardens can be a bit like a maze especially after dusk."

"Not at all, Mariana. Mr. Smyth and I were in a philosophical conversation and lost track of time." Turning to Thomas. "Mr. Smyth, I thank you for your time and your perspective. You have given me quite a bit to think about. If you will excuse us, we really should be heading back inside."

"Of course, my lady. My apologies for keeping you out so late. I should have kept better track of the hour." He bowed. "My lady, Mrs. Jacobson, Mr. Gillam." The three of them turned and headed back inside.

I do not remember a more profitable tea party. My compliments to Lady Kelt, he thought.

CHAPTER FIVE

Daniel Crossings was not uncomfortable with clandestine meetings. He'd spent the majority of his adult life in dark, rat-infested places, tending to business. As the man of business to the seventh Count Trenton, one of the most corrupt miscreants ever to disgrace this earth, Daniel had seen every level of depravity known to man. What he did object to was stupidity. It was bad enough having to work under the thumb of his current employer, the eighth Count of Trenton; it seems he now had to share his time between two incompetent idiots: the aforementioned count and his addlepated brother-in-law, the Marquess of Walsenburg.

"Good evening, my lord. With all due respect, do you think it best to meet in your coach to discuss our affairs? Your family crest on the doors makes us rather conspicuous, would you not agree?" Well, that didn't sound so bad. If this fool could only read his thoughts.

George Hastings waved his hand as if sweeping Daniel's concerns away. "Nonsense. We certainly cannot meet at my residence to discuss these matters. And I refuse to set foot in those flea-infested dens you frequent. Heaven knows what disease you may walk away with if you are fortunate enough not to be bludgeoned to death by some inebriated ruffian."

Very well. The risk was minimal to Daniel. He was nothing more than a paid servant. If this dandy wanted to forgo security for comfort, so be it. "I have received word regarding the *Prospero*. The ship is being held for ransom by local pirates. They demand ten thousand in gold and silver, or they will sell the cargo and crew for a profit and burn the ship."

"This is preposterous! There is over twenty-five thousand in cargo on that vessel alone. If it does not dock in Salassio within a week's time, I will be ruined. What have you heard from Trenton?"

"Not a word, my lord. As you know, he is on his honeymoon with the new Lady Trenton and has not responded to my missives." It wasn't a complete lie. Daniel had sent his employer three encrypted messages informing him of the situation. The problem was that he had sent them to the count's Salassio residence on Bellstrand. There was little possibility Count Trenton would see them prior to his return at month's end.

"Ten thousand in gold and silver! When is the ransom due?"

"They gave us until two nights hence, my lord." Daniel waited anxiously for George's reply. He knew this would push the marquess past his capabilities. He'd have to seek financial backing elsewhere.

"Make the arrangements. I will come up with the funding. Get out!" With that he almost physically pushed Daniel from the coach while tapping on the roof for the driver to proceed.

Daniel wasted little time in making his way to Tenison's secret offices in the dodgier part of Salassio's peasant district.

Entering the small, musty pub, Daniel removed his coat. He took a quick assessment of the room, and noting nothing and no one out of place, he proceeded to the back corner and straight into the office of his real employer.

Teddy sat hidden in the shadows and presumably well in his cups when Daniel walked in. He recognized Daniel immediately. This was the conduit between Walsenburg and Tenison. He could now confirm the relationship and the danger, which was closer than anyone predicted. They had to move, and they had to move fast.

CHAPTER SIX

There was a loud knock at the door. Who could this be at the break of dawn? Moreover, no one knew where he lived. Thomas picked up the boot dagger he kept next to his bed and approached the door quietly. "Who knocks?"

"Open up, Smyth, before I wake your very curious neighbors."

Thomas instantly recognized Teddy's voice. "What has happened to bring you here and at this hour of the day?"

"Walsenburg is being pressured for additional capital. The estimate is between ten and fifteen thousand within the next two days. He cannot come up with that amount on his own. He will be forced to borrow funds."

"There are only three options open to him. Friends, family, or a moneylender. He does not have many friends, and the ones he has cannot or will not meet the demands. The only moneylender with those resources is Tenison, and he is the one extorting the gold. All he has left is family. And the only family member with enough coin is his mother, the dowager marchioness." Thomas had to think fast. *How do I get to her fortune before Junior?*

"Thomas, there is something you are not telling me. Would you care to share?" Working with Thomas for the past three years had made Teddy wise to his partner's changes in expression.

"I received word from my sources delving into the dowager marchioness's net worth." Thomas went to the small desk by the window and handed Teddy a three-page letter. "The late Duke and Duchess of Colton were heavily invested in mining and shipping. In the past ten years, most of the profits from both enterprises have been used in buying up mass parcels of land and property in various kingdoms including Sonastare. Although the details are still being deciphered, the estate is worth a king's ransom and may make its heir wealthier than the royal family several times over."

"Wait just a moment. How is this even possible? His Grace's estate was settled over a year ago. You remember the gossip well. The title went to his closest living male heir, his nephew Gregory Marlborough, the twelfth and current Duke of Colton, along with the entailed property and assets. Everything else not directly linked to the duchy, was left to their only daughter Lady Analisa Elizabeth Childress-Hastings, the then Marchioness of Walsenburg. There was no mention or even a rumor of additional interests. This cannot be accurate."

"Not only is it true; it is most probable." Thomas grabbed the papers from Teddy's hands. "There is a small and relatively insignificant barony in Artemisia few have ever heard of for decades if not centuries. The twelfth Baron of Pennington died without issue or male heir over fourteen years past. His closest living heir was a grand-niece by the name of Elizabeth Forsyth. Since there are no restrictions that the line must continue through the next legitimate male heir, Elizabeth Forsyth became the thirteenth Baroness Pennington."

"Elizabeth Forsyth-Childress was Analisa's mother, and the then Duchess of Colton. But how did this relatively obsucure barony amass such a vast fortune?"

"The eleventh Duke of Colton was a very savvy businessman. He knew that upon his death, the title would go to his nephew, and since they were not close, he had little confidence his wife and children would be provided for. About ten years ago he began divesting personal funds from his unentailed portfolio to the barony in Artemisia. All business was conducted privately through his duchess and with a very discreet man of business in Artemisia by the name of Miles Granger. The duke refused to take any capital out of the barony's portfolio for fear of alerting anyone to his wife's Artemisian title. As you well know, there remain animosities between our two kingdoms after the Millennial Wars."

"The animosity is emotional. There are no laws preventing Sonastarians from holding titles in both kingdoms. Lord Bixby is a perfect example of this. He is a count in Sonastare and holds a viscountcy in Artemisia on his mother's side."

"That was never the issue. The late duke simply wanted to protect his daughter. Since no funds were ever drawn and all profits reinvested wisely, the once destitute barony grew to become an enormous fortune."

"If this becomes public knowledge…"

"Exactly!" Thomas raked his fingers through his hair in frustration. "Although she remains completely unaware, Lady Analisa Elizabeth Childress-Hastings, Dowager Marchioness of Walsenburg, is the Current fourteenth Baroness Pennington and an extremely wealthy woman in her own right."

"Are you certain this information has not been made public?"

"I am certain of it. The goings-on in Artemisia are of little concern to Sonastare, and the Artemisian parliament believes the current Baroness of Pennington to be a recluse but living somewhere on one of her many estates. Mr. Granger files all of the necessary paperwork to satisfy the Artemisian officials of her health and active participation in barony affairs."

"Thomas, this will not remain a secret for long. Once this is released, our little pigeon becomes fair game for every fortune hunter in the world. We need to get there first. What are you planning to do?"

"Simple. I plan to marry the lady before the information goes public."

CHAPTER SEVEN

"**M**y lady, Mr. Ryan DelCroft to see you." Powers executed an exaggerated bow fit to honor an empress. Analisa was always flattered but concerned. Roger Powers was well over sixty years of age. He'd been butler to the Colton duchy since his father retired from the position when Powers was two and twenty. He had served her grandfather and her father. Once her father died, the new duke brought in his own staff and Powers was retired. Not long after, the Walsenburg butler, too, decided to retire, and Analisa offered Powers the position. Due to his advanced years he was not really expected to do much, other than supervise the enormous staff maintaining the Walsenburg family estate. There were three under butlers assigned to make sure Powers did not overextend himself. When Analisa retired to the dowager house, Powers was one of the retainers she brought with her. The fact is the man was completely devoted to her and her family. In fact, for Analisa, the dowager house staff was her family.

Mr. DelCroft entered and paused a moment while Powers exited and closed the doors behind him. "Ana! You are looking as beautiful as ever."

Analisa extended her arms to him, hugging and bussing his cheeks with genuine affection. "Ryan. You have been singing my praises since we were eight. At some point I will become less beautiful and just plain old."

"Never! That tragedy could never befall you." He refused to let go of her until the absolute last moment. "I will not stand for anyone using that word in reference to you. Not even you." He could always make her laugh.

"Very well, how about a compromise? Once my wrinkles become more prominent and my hair loses its shine, we describe me as 'radiant' or 'enchanting'?"

"Done and done, but you will always be beautiful to me. The pox could not change that."

"Good heavens! Anything but that!" She linked arms with him in the most intimate way. "Come. Let us have some coffee, or tea if you would prefer, and let us catch up."

The fact was that Ryan DelCroft and Analisa had grown up together without concern for rank or status. Ryan's father had been the curator of Sonastare's art museum for over thirty years. He and the late Duke of Colton were good friends, and shared a passion for the arts, particularly oil on canvas.

Growing up as the son of the curator of one of the most impressive art galleries in the world, Ryan became a foremost authority of modern art by the time he reached his sixteenth year. He had read every book and publication printed regarding art and art history and could tell a particular artist's brush stroke on sight. At one and twenty, he announced he had learned all there was to learn about art in Sonastare and wished to travel the world in an effort to enhance and broaden his education. His family was well endowed but unable to finance years of study abroad. At this point the Duke of Colton stepped in and offered Ryan the position as artistic agent to the Colton duchy. For the next several years, Ryan traveled the world collecting knowledge as well as art, which he shipped back for display at the art museum or for private collections—most notably, that of the Duke of Colton.

The world was an amazing place, but nothing could ever entice him enough to leave Sonastare behind. How could it? Only Sonastare had Analisa Childress, and Analisa Childress had his heart.

"So, tell me, my friend, what has you up and about at this unfashionable hour of the morning?"

"I sail for the continent on the evening tide. Several ancient artifacts were uncovered in a dig in South Africa. From what little I have been able to gather; it may be a burial site dating back to the fourteenth century. The information is perplexing since they have uncovered several sculptures, weapons, and ornamentation not commonly found in graves regardless of affluence. I need to assess the site personally to make sense of it all." These mysteries always excited him. He tried to make it sound like a scientific venture purely for academic enlightenment, but he was fooling no one. Least of all Analisa.

"And how long will you be gone for this latest adventure?"

"It is not an adventure, Ana. What we find can prove historically significant for generations to come. The artwork alone could prove priceless."

"Do you know your eyes light up when you are on the verge of a new quest? Like a little boy with a brand-new puzzle to solve on Christmas morning." She looked around as if just remembering something. "Speaking of Christmas, I have something for you." She rose and slowly walked over to the elaborately ornate Baroque cabinet adorning the north wall of the morning room. He really was a little boy at times. Although he tried to act very mature and nonchalant, she knew that inside he was anxiously anticipating what the gift might be. They'd been playing this game since they were children. The first gift he had ever given her was when they were both very young. He'd presented her with an enormous opal he'd uncovered while on safari in the attic of the museum's annex. Wrapping it in a silk handkerchief, Ryan had offered it to her the week before her eighth birthday. She had never seen anything so beautiful. Brilliant, genuine, and shining

41

just for her. That was how she remembered his face, his expression as he handed her the stone.

Of course, the opal was not actually an opal. It was a lovely colored stone that had fallen off one of the museum's discarded statues. But to Analisa, it was Ryan. Her father had encouraged the romantic illusion, showering praise and astonishment over the incredibly valuable piece. He went so far as to have it set into a cameo-style necklace for her to keep and cherish. That "opal" was Ryan. To the world, it was just another pretty rock, but to her…

From the bottom drawer of the chest, she took out a heavy box. She took a moment, smiling mischievously, knowing the anticipation would be driving him mad.

Walking over to where he sat, she handed him the box. "This is not really a present nor is it in commemoration of any particular event." He took the box from her slowly, never taking his eyes off hers. "It belonged to my father. But to be honest, I have always felt it belonged to you and merely on loan to him for safekeeping. It is only right it should be returned to its rightful owner."

Carefully Ryan unwrapped the box. Opening it, he discovered a beautifully detailed sculpture of an ancient Greek manticore. Considered a highly dangerous beast with the head of a man, the body of a lion, and the tail of a scorpion, the piece was straight out of mythological folklore. It was six inches in height and expertly sculptured in jade. The duke had purchased it from an impoverished young woman many years before. The girl looked to be in dire straits and His Grace felt sorry for the waif.

For many years it sat on the duke's desk. Ryan had admired it since he first laid eyes on it as a child. His father had brought him along on one of his visits to Chateau Montpellier, the duke's residence on Bellstrand. It was this statue that had piqued his interest in art. It was what launched his career.

"Ana. I do not know what to say. This is much too valuable a gift.

I should not accept it. Are you certain you would not rather save it for your son or grandson some day?"

"You will accept it as it is not so much a gift from me as it is an inheritance from the late Duke of Colton. I know in my heart he would have wanted it for you. Please accept it."

"I do accept, as I will treasure it always." He took a moment to clear his throat and his vision. "Now. Where were we. Oh yes. I should be gone through the season if all goes well. It is a long journey there and back, and I am not sure how much time it will take to authenticate and catalog the findings."

When the maid brought in a tray of coffee and some freshly baked goods, Ryan turned his face toward the window. He was becoming concerned over his growing feelings for Ana. Did everyone who looked at him know? Not possible. With over thirty years of practice concealing his feelings for her, he was a more accomplished actor than anyone on stage today. He was a witness at her wedding to the marquess, for heaven's sake. If he didn't break then, he would not break now or ever.

"Here you are. Light cream, no sugar, as you prefer it." She presented him with a small tray of assorted sweets. "These are also very lightly sweetened. After all these years, even Cook has perfected a treat for your palate that will not overwhelm."

He took a lemon cake. Not too sugary but with the perfect balance of tart and sweet. "Please convey my compliments to Mrs. Parker. These are perfect."

They spoke for an hour or so of mundane things, happy to be enjoying some quiet time together.

"Have you heard from the new Countess Trenton? I would imagine she is deliriously happy."

"Nothing from Evie since they left. I am sure she is happy although I would argue my children do not know the meaning of 'delirious' let alone what it may feel like to be overtaken by the emotion."

"I take it George has set up permanent residence in mild satisfaction or has he risen to a weak level of contentment?"

"Dear George. I do not believe he will ever be content under any circumstances. However, there is something going on behind the façade. I do not know if it is tangible or emotional, but I wish he would share his concerns with me. I know I can help him if only he would allow it."

Ryan reached out to gently cover her hand with his. "Ana, do not forget he is not a little boy any longer. He is a man, and a titled one at that. You and his late father gave him love, encouragement, and a solid education; and I am not talking academics. I speak of life." He closed his palm and squeezed a little tighter. "What he is and what he will become from this point onward is completely within his control."

"He is my son, Ryan. He will never stop being my son nor I his mother. I am afraid worry comes with that title as well."

"Well, it is time I depart. I must make some last-minute arrangements before we sail this evening." He stood, bowed, and kissed her hand. "Promise you will miss me terribly."

Analisa sprang to her feet, enveloping him in a tight and desperate hug. "I already do, you greedy man. Leaving me for some old rocks and dirt." She stepped back to take a good look at him before he left. "Please promise me you will be careful, and that you will be back soon?"

"As if some old rocks could keep me away." He released her and walked toward the doors. "Ancient frescos, now that would be a different matter altogether."

Please bring him home safely, Lord. The same prayer she'd been reciting countless times each year since he began feeding his wanderlust. *I cannot lose him as well. I would not have the strength to survive it.*

CHAPTER EIGHT

"Are we prepared for this evening?" Thomas was just putting on his evening jacket as Teddy entered his rooms.

"We are as ready as we will ever be. I wish we had had more time to prepare. I do not like these rush jobs. There is too much room for error."

"Think of it as a challenge to our ability to think on our feet. Our past exploits have all been methodically worked out. Minimal risk with maximum reward. This one will test our mettle."

"Easy for you to say. You can simply disappear like smoke if things go heinously awry. I, on the other hand, will likely find myself dancing at the end of a hangman's rope before my next birthday."

Thomas walked over and braced Teddy by the shoulders. "Buck up, old man. We have everything under control." He walked to the door and opened it to leave as casually as if doing no more than taking an evening stroll. "Be on time and in place by the appointed hour. All will be well." He left a frustrated and angry Teddy to ponder the pitfalls of this crazy endeavor all alone. "Devil take the man. Why can he not simply accept his life and circumstances like the rest of us? You cannot pick your family or your social status. God does that for you, and many believe He has a plan. If this goes wrong, I am sure I will have the chance to ask Him personally. I may be screaming a long way up, but I will ask."

Salassio's Museum of Art was an architectural masterpiece. It was designed after the Parthenon in Athens, only three times the size. The columns were hand-crafted marble with most of the building and surrounding properties reengineered to reflect how the ancient building in Athens would have looked in its first few years of life. Of course, there were no pictures of the time, so artists, architects, and engineers had to guess at much of what was. And with some of the deepest pockets in the world funding the project, a great deal of liberty was taken to present one of the most aesthetically beautiful yet secure edifices in the world.

Rumors abounded of secret rooms and compartments designed to protect the artwork if in danger. There were multiple escape tunnels and an army of dedicated soldiers trained and committed to the protection of the museum and its content.

There were even rumors of a museum within the museum. Rooms where only the rarest of all art was stored and displayed for the top 1 percent of the Elite. The 1 percent of the 1 percent. This included approximately eleven families in all Sonastare.

Thomas's leased coach followed the parade of conveyances as they dropped their privileged cargo off at the main entrance.

The season was just getting under way with the museum's annual ball as one of the keystones. If this ball was a success, all that followed would be, likewise, successful. A bad opening ball would cast a cloud over the entire season. This only served to put the audience on their very best behavior. In over two hundred years this event had gone off to perfection. Those present made sure of it.

Thomas looked around with a contented sigh. If all went as planned, tonight would be another magnificent triumph for the museum, and for Sonastare. If anything went wrong, there would be a heavy price to pay. "Oh well." He ran a hand over his hair, and then over his coat and trousers. "Once more unto the breach, dear friends, once more."

This time his name had been added to the guest list courtesy of Lady Kelt and the Duchess of Welby. Thomas was announced, and immediately proceeded to establish his alibi. He needed to make certain as many of the Elite as possible would, and could, vouch for his whereabouts throughout the evening. This was essential to his mission's success if the plan failed. Just a precaution but a wise one given the consequences.

"Good evening, my ladies." Thomas approached a group of matrons. Amongst them, Baroness Kelt, the Duchess of Welby, Viscountess Cross, and Mrs. Jacobson. "Your Grace, my ladies, Mrs. Jacobson; you are all visions this evening as you have been at every encounter."

"Mr. Smyth, how good of you to join us. I hope you are prepared to be impressed. We have some of the rarest works of art in the world within these walls. If not impressed, you will certainly not be disappointed."

"Nothing about this visit has been even remotely disappointing, Your Grace. Please excuse me. I am off to take advantage of this opening salvo to take a quick tour before the crush disperses."

"Of course. Please do not hesitate to reach out if you have any questions. Most of us have an extensive knowledge of the museum's content and would be delighted to share what we know."

With a quick bow to no lady in particular, Thomas made his way to the southernmost corner of the main gallery, where the refreshment tables had been set up. Along the way he greeted several acquaintances and was introduced to important members of society. Now all he had to do was wait.

Almost one hour had passed when she was announced. "Lady Analisa Hastings, Dowager Marchioness of Walsenburg."

Most looked to the top of the stairs as Analisa descended to the main salon. She was wearing a gown of sky-blue silk that fit her to perfection. Her shoulders bare, with long, white silk gloves accenting the brilliance of the diamond bracelet she wore. Her hair was up in a fashionable coif but without the garish adornments ladies of a certain age seem to favor. Breathtaking. She would be impossible to duplicate and deceive those who knew her. Fortunately, the ones they had to mislead were not acquainted with the marchioness. They weren't even within reach of this strata in society.

Viscountess Cross met her halfway across the room. "My dear! How lovely you look."

"Thank you, Maggie. Am I the last to arrive?"

"Of our circle, yes. But I do not see Walsenburg in the audience. Will he and the marchioness be attending this evening?"

"I was told they would be attending. It would be in very poor taste if they failed to make an appearance."

"Come along. The ladies have been asking for you." Maggie looked around conspiratorially. "Mr. Smyth arrived just a few minutes ago. What a handsome man he is. It is a shame and a miracle he is unattached. His looks alone are enough to melt any heart including those of stone and ice." Maggie stopped Analisa just short of joining the group. "The two of you spoke in the garden at Marie's tea on Bellstrand a few days ago. Did he mention his family or his background? No one seems to know much about him except that he is as beautifully sculptured as any statue in this mausoleum. I meant museum."

"No, we did not discuss his family at all. He was a kind man who stepped in to distract me when he saw my sadness at Walsenburg's entrance.

"I will never understand why you find it necessary to besmirch the solemnity of this establishment. Your family has been a proud and devoted patron of Salassio's Museum of Art since its opening."

"It is not the museum itself I disdain per se. It is simply that everything in this magnificent building is so old. Why are the accumulation of years envied in art but not in people? I tell you it is not fair. Moreover, why not introduce modern art into the inventory? Not everything old is beautiful and not everything new is ugly." Maggie was becoming more agitated and so she stopped. "Enough of my capricious biases. We are here to enjoy our evening. Come along."

All that beauty and all that wealth. Quite a tempting catch for any enterprising young man looking for an easy life.

Thomas gave her a quarter of an hour to gab with her friends before approaching. He brought Malcolm along to minimize any fear of a predatory threat. He also suggested they bring the ladies some lemonade. They must be parched by now.

"Good evening, my lady." He greeted Analisa specifically since she was the only one who had joined the group since his last appearance. "We thought you would all appreciate some light refreshments. The evening is warm and the presence of so many only helps to elevate the temperature."

The footman who followed them with a full tray stepped forward. Thomas and Malcolm did the honors, personally presenting each lady with a glass of cool lemonade.

"Handsome and very well mannered. How have you managed to remain unattached, Mr. Smyth?" The Duchess of Welby smiled as she accepted the glass he offered.

"You have only been exposed to my gentlemanly traits, Your Grace. As with all men, we have many we keep hidden that would make us a much less coveted prize."

"My dear Mr. Smyth. Perfection is only rarely assumed and never a probability. It is a man's imperfection that necessitates a wife. And vice versa."

"Please go on, Your Grace. You have me intrigued. Is the goal not to secure the perfect mate?"

"Only when we are young and naïve. For with youth comes ignorance, ideology, and denial. With age comes experience and acceptance and, ultimately, if you are very good and very fortunate, happiness and love. Trust me when I tell you that in the game of life, we are attracted to beauty, but it is always the flaws we fall in love with."

Analisa felt a bit lightheaded. "Dear? Are you all right? You have gone absolutely pale." Maggie reached out to gently support Analisa, helping her to the nearest chair.

"Oh dear. It must be the heat in the room. I do feel a little out of sorts."

"Here, have a little bit more to drink. It should help to cool you off."

Analisa took another sip of the lemonade. The dizziness subsided but she still felt over warm.

"Perhaps a stroll on the terrace. The air is much cooler there and the breeze will help bring your color back."

"I would be happy to escort Lady Walsenburg to the terrace." Thomas looked hopeful and the lady accommodated.

"Thank you, Mr. Smyth, I would be very grateful."

Thomas extended his arm, and leaning on his strength to a greater extent than was appropriate, Analisa rose. "I am so terribly sorry to be a bother. I enjoy the strongest of constitutions. I cannot remember the last time I fell ill. It must be this heat. You are very kind to accompany me. I hope I am not keeping you."

"Not at all. I would greatly enjoy your company. I only regret it is under diminished circumstances."

They walked slowly toward the terrace doors. There were a few people taking in the fresh air but most were still deep in conversations and refreshments.

"Is Mr. DelCroft here this evening? I would have thought this is one event he would not miss."

"Sadly no, Mr. DelCroft is off to South Africa on an archeological mission. He did, however, have much to do with the arrangement for this evening's events. He is also responsible for most of the artwork in the museum as his travels have afforded him the opportunity of collecting some of the rarest pieces from all over the world. So, in point of fact, he is here even as he is not."

"I have often wondered if a person can be in two places at once. I believe you have resolved that dilemma. Thank you."

Out on the terrace they quickly found an empty bench where Analisa could rest and enjoy the cool breeze. "That feels very refreshing." She closed her eyes, taking a deep, cleansing breath. "Would you care to sit down, Mr. Smyth? We should not be long."

Thomas took the seat next to her. They spoke for a few minutes until Analisa felt recuperated. "Shall we rejoin the festivities?"

Thomas stood and reached down for her hand to assist her to her feet. "Must we return so soon? The night is lovely, and the tours have not yet commenced. Would you mind a stroll in the east gardens before we rejoin the crush?"

"Not at all but we must not dally. I can tell you this, our curator prides himself on punctuality and a strict schedule. He would never forgive us if we joined the tour after it began."

They made their way toward the stone steps leading down to the formal gardens. There were lamps lit along the path and several stone benches carefully positioned giving both privacy and respite to adventurous guests.

They'd walked to the far side of the east gardens when two men joined them coming out from behind the trees just ahead of them.

They were dressed in dark clothing and had disguised their faces so they could not be recognized. "What is the meaning of this? Who are you?" Thomas demanded.

"We ain't the royal guard, Your Lordship," the taller of the two mocked. "Now, be good little children and don't make this more difficult than it has to be."

With that, a third man came up behind them, draped a sack over Analisa's head, and bound her hands behind her.

She was terrified and disoriented when a voice came very near her ear. "My lady. I know you are frightened, and I must apologize for bringing this upon you, but I assure you, it is quite necessary. We have no intentions of harming you in any way, at least not more than what we have already done. Please do not resist and I promise, you will be treated with great respect while in our care."

Analisa had never been abducted before, but she'd read books and true-to-life accounts of kidnappings, and this is not what she would have expected.

Her abductor gently guided her forward by the shoulders. He assisted her into what was obviously a coach and saw to her comfort in the conveyance. "I will untie your hands so you may be more comfortable. Please do not struggle and please do not remove the hood covering your face. It is for your own protection that you do not know where we are taking you. Again, you have my word you will not be harmed. Do you understand?"

She wasn't sure how she was to respond, so she simply nodded her head in agreement.

The coach ride took several hours. Once darkness fell, she was allowed to remove her hood. The windows had all been covered and her companions maintained their disguises. She did not know who they were, where they were headed, or why she'd become a target, but she felt her best chances for survival was to do as she was told. At least for the time being.

The coach stopped at a remote residence by the coast. She could smell the sea.

"My lady, I must have you replace your hood for the final leg of our journey. We will be making a short crossing on a small vessel. It will not be a long journey and you will be perfectly safe. Do you understand?"

This time she responded more confidently. "Yes, I understand."

Her captors did not communicate verbally. They must have been communicating through gestures or designed this abduction to such detail, words were superfluous. Several things were clear. These men were well trained. She'd heard no names, places, and could identify neither her captors nor her location. She would make a terrible spy for the crown.

Making jokes at a time like this, Ana? she scolded herself. No, it wasn't funny, but so far they had treated her well. The joke must have been some sort of defense mechanism. That was all.

They assisted her carefully into a small rowboat. Three others boarded with her, and they began rowing toward some unknown destination. Unknown to her in any event.

Several minutes later the small boat came to a sudden stop, making contact with a hard object. More than likely some sort of dock, she assumed.

"Before we disembark, I will need your ring, my lady." Analisa wore an exquisite ten-karat, pear-shaped emerald ring with a double diamond halo all set in fine gold. It was priceless.

"My ring? Why? It is of little worth other than the sentimental value it holds for me. My husband gave it to me as a promise ring, and I have not had it off my finger since I accepted his suit."

"I would argue its worth is far greater than you realize, my lady. However, I assure you it will be returned to you in a few days." He reached down and gently slipped the ring from her finger. "I will help you up, my lady." Gentle but strong hands assisted her up. "There will be three steps immediately in front of you. The first is rather high. Please be very careful as you find your footing. I will be right here to make sure you do not get hurt."

"I have never been abducted before this evening, sir. Are all abductions this amicable?"

Her companion must have smiled for she heard the humor in his voice as he responded.

"Since this is my first abduction as well, I must confess I have little experience on which to base an opinion."

"We may consider collaborating on a book outlining the experience from each of our perspectives. It may prove to be a best seller." Why was she bantering with this man? He took her by force and was about to do God knows what to her. She should be terrified. Shouldn't she? This was all very confusing.

They walked up a slight incline and into a building. She heard the door close behind them. "I will remove your hood now, my lady." He gently lifted the silk cowl from her head. There was little light, but enough to see a modest home tastefully furnished and warm.

Her companion went around the room lighting more candles, showing more and more of the tasteful decor and above average comforts of the lodging.

"If you will have a seat, my lady, I will do my best to answer what questions you may have."

She sat down at one of the armchairs closest to the fire. The evening was warm, but they were somewhere by the sea and she was probably in shock. The fire felt comforting.

Her captor stood somewhere behind her between shadow and light. "I would first request you give me a name."

This was nothing like anything she had ever read about. "That is an odd request, sir. Do you not already have a name?"

"I do indeed, my lady. Unfortunately, it would not be safe to share that name with you. If you would provide me with a name to which I will answer the few times I am in your presence, everything will work out much more smoothly."

"I am at a loss, sir." And a bit confused.

"Think back to when you met someone for the first time. They were introduced as John and you thought to yourself, 'You do not strike me as a John. You look more like a…'"

"Iago!" The name just jumped into her head.

"Othello's villain. May I ask why Iago?"

"It is the one that came to mind. He was a villain, true, but he was also a tormented soul. Not all good but not all bad. That is how I would describe you in what little time we have shared."

"Then I am humbled and flattered, my lady. Iago I am."

"The first thing I need to know is where is Mr. Smyth? He was not brought with us. Has he been harmed?"

"Mr. Smyth has not been harmed, but we found it necessary to separate you for reasons I cannot share. I can assure you; he has suffered no detriment at our hands."

"I have little choice but to take you at your word. So tell me, my misunderstood Iago, why am I here?"

"Unfortunately, that is one piece of information I cannot share with you at this time, my lady."

"Very well, what can you tell me?"

"You are an extraordinary lady with a life much more complicated than you have been led to believe. You have been brought here for a short while as part of orchestrating an illusion designed to benefit a select but important few. While you are with us, you will have a small staff who will cater to your every need within reason. You will need to assign them names as you have done for me." He paused to gauge her mood. So far, so good. "Once the stage has been set, you will be returned home to step into your role."

"And who am I to be, pray tell?"

"You will be you, my lady, but under altered circumstances."

"Altered circumstances?"

"I am afraid that is another bit of information I am not at liberty to discuss with you at this time."

"Let me ask you this. Will any of this bring harm to me or my family or friends? Will any of this harm their lives or reputation in any way?"

"There is no plan to harm anyone but there may be some harmful if unforeseen fallout. Unfortunately, we cannot orchestrate a reaction to our actions."

"Is there anything I can do or say to bring a swift end to these theatrics? I can pay you. Name your price."

"I am only a spoke in the wheel, my lady. I do not have the authority to make that decision, but I will pass your offer along to my master."

"So, you are not the one in charge?"

"No, my lady. My master is in the process of setting the stage as we speak."

CHAPTER NINE

"Thomas!" Malcolm seemed agitated and a bit frightened. "Have you seen the Lady Walsenburg of late? My mother and her friends are beside themselves with worry."

"I have not, my friend. Last I saw her, she was coming in from the terrace, rejuvenated and ready to rejoin the festivities."

"Apparently she never made it back. The ladies have the entire museum staff looking for the marchioness."

"Can I be of assistance? I would be happy to join the search if you feel it will help."

"No need at this time. She may have decided to return to Bellstrand. Her coach is gone, and someone said they may have seen her leaving through the side door."

"I am at your disposal. Please feel free to call on me at any time."

"Thank you, Thomas. I must return to the ladies to see how goes the search."

The evening was coming to an end. Although there were some questions surrounding the marchioness's absence, the light uproar seemed to have calmed. Thomas headed for the door. Being one of the few left at the museum, it didn't take long for his coach to be brought around. He headed straight for his lodgings, where he knew Teddy would be waiting.

Opening the door to his leased rooms, he found Teddy literally at the edge of his seat.

"So? How did it go?"

"Alexander and his team brought Her Ladyship to the cabin as planned. The distress signal was not activated, so we must assume the lady is well nested on the island."

"Good. I have no doubt Alexander has things well in hand. By morning, the alert will be out that the lady did not return home, triggering a citywide panic. A search crew will be organized."

"We have arranged to have six reports coming in that the lady has been seen at different locations throughout Sonastare. One will even have her boarding a ship to South Africa." Teddy yawned.

"Sailing toward Mr. Ryan DelCroft? That is a bit scandalous, would you not agree?"

"Not really since she is not actually on a ship south. But it will allow for honest speculation and it makes for good theater."

"Well, what is done is done. I will join in the search as soon as it escalates. What of our lookalike?"

"Her name is Miriam Vernon. She has the same body type as the marchioness. Her hair color can be easily altered but her mannerisms and speech are too crude to be believable."

Thomas had already considered this. "She will be weakened by her ordeal. We will teach her some basic responses and mannerisms, limiting her interactions to the bare minimum. The only time she will need to interact at all will be at Mariposa, and that will be for only a few minutes with a handful of people." Thomas kept thinking of any vulnerabilities they'd not considered.

"Did you secure a special license?" Teddy had to ask since without it all this would be for not.

"I did indeed." Thomas grinned like the tomcat who after many attempts has finally cornered the juiciest hen in the hen-house. "In less than a fortnight Mr. Thomas Smyth will be the fourteenth Baron Pennington and a very, very wealthy baron indeed."

CHAPTER TEN

It wasn't long after sunup when word came down that the dowager marchioness of Walsenburg was missing. The city was in an uproar. One of their most prominent citizens had disappeared. The problem was that this was all anyone knew. There was no evidence of foul play, and thus far news that she'd been spotted in three different locations on opposite sides of the kingdom were having a terribly detrimental and confusing effect on the search.

The crown had been notified and resources had been extended to the local authorities.

Thomas waited for the frenzy to escalate to a respectable level before making his way to Miramarea Abbey on Bellstrand. Though the rules of exclusivity remained, admittance by invitation only, Thomas approached the same chief steward he'd met on his first visit to the island. It wasn't difficult to convince the man he was there to help, and was granted passage to cross.

Miramarea Abbey was bustling. The local authorities were present but so were the royal guard and the Bellstrand militia. As he entered, he was immediately sequestered and interrogated.

"Officers, please, desist this attack instantly!" Lady Kelt came in from the hall flailing her arms as if swatting flies. "This young man is a close friend of the dowager marchioness. If he is here, he is here to help." She linked her arm with Thomas's. "Come with me, young man."

She escorted him down the hall to the family sitting rooms. Walsenburg and his wife were present as was the Duchess of Welby and Viscountess Cross. There were a few others he had not met, but everyone seemed to be focusing on the duchess for guidance.

"Walsenburg, what are you going to do about this? You have the resources at your disposal, but they require direction. You must provide that direction NOW!"

Ada, Duchess of Welby, was not one to mince words and she was obviously very agitated and more than a little angry at Walsenburg's lack of initiative.

"What direction am I to provide, Your Grace?" He looked disoriented and fearful. "She is missing but we do not know the circumstances surrounding her absence. They may be voluntary."

"Do you really believe your mother would abandon her home and family even for a day without giving notice and without a moment's preparation?" She stared at him almost forcing him to respond. The man's expression was impassive. She'd had enough of this fool.

"Collinsworth!" A middle-aged yet severe-looking man stepped forward. "You are the authority on Bellstrand. You are taking charge of the search. Until my husband returns, you will report to this committee every detail of your plan and progress."

"Of course, Your Grace." He turned to the handful of men just behind him. "Gather the heads of the Royal Guard and the Sonastarian reserve forces. I will meet with them in my office in ten minutes. Gather the volunteer force in the public forum, we will join you there with further instructions within the hour."

Thomas secured transportation for himself to the public forum and awaited further orders.

An hour later Collinsworth stood before over one hundred

volunteers gathered in the public forum. "Gentlemen, we will be separating you into teams accompanying official authorities in conducting a detailed search for Lady Walsenburg. We will be addressing the obvious initially, but we will turn our attentions to the remote if we are unsuccessful with our initial efforts. If you feel you may know where to look, I would encourage you to take the initiative but please keep in communications with Bellstrand authorities. That is all."

Dismissed, Thomas took his leave of the forum and the island. He'd return to Salassio, pick up what few necessities he required, and be on his way.

Everything was coming together according to plan.

CHAPTER ELEVEN

A Hidden Island Manor in Sonastare

Iago, or rather Alexander, docked his small rowboat by the island's lagoon. He disembarked and made a quick assessment of the environment. Two days had passed since he'd been here and he had just returned bearing supplies and to check on Lady Walsenburg.

He was greeted outside of the cottage by the armed guard who opened the door for him. Inside the antechamber, he picked up one of the various masks on the table and carefully secured it in place, using the mirror to verify it firmly concealed his identity. He knocked on the parlor door and was admitted by a house maid. "Good afternoon, Mr. Iago. I hope you had an uneventful crossing."

"Good afternoon, Desdemona. And how is our guest faring this fine day?"

"Why not ask me directly, Mr. Iago?" Analisa entered the small home's main chamber from her sitting room.

Alexander gave her a respectful bow. "Good day, my lady. Are you well?"

"I am well, sir, but growing increasingly frustrated. Any word on when I may be released from my gilded cage?"

"Not yet, my lady, but soon. The performance is progressing on schedule and very soon you will be required to reenter the stage."

"How mysterious." She walked to the table she used for her meals and other mundane purposes. "Will you join me for tea, Mr. Iago? I would welcome the company."

"I would be honored, my lady." He helped her to her seat and took the chair opposite her at the table. "I must commend you on your composure during these trying times. Any other woman would have melted into hysterics by now."

"I will not deny that I have been tempted on more than one occasion, Mr. Iago. And I may yet before this play is over. However, hysterics never solves problems; it typically makes matters worse. Besides, you and your colleagues have treated me well over the last few days and nights." Desdemona placed the tea service before Analisa. "Should I do the honors, sir?"

"If you would not mind, my lady."

Analisa poured and handed him a cup. "May I ask what has been communicated to my family regarding my whereabouts? They must be frantic with worry."

"Sadly, my lady, their worry could not be prevented. There is in fact a frantic search in progress to find you."

"And will that search be successful?"

"I am afraid not, my lady." He looked genuinely remorseful. "You will be found safe and unharmed but by my master and on cue. Not a moment before."

"Very well, if that is your will. So be it."

"Not my will, my lady, but I must see this charade through to the end. To quote Sergey Nechayev, 'the end justifies the means.'"

"I do hope for all of our sakes that you are correct, Mr. Iago."

CHAPTER TWELVE

The Small City of Mariposa, Artemisia

"Miss me?" Thomas walked into Willow House's private dining room in Mariposa windblown and dusty, but still more handsome than any man had a right to be.

"Should we have?" Teddy was bored, frustrated, and irritable. He'd spent the last three days cooped up with Ms. Miriam Vernon at Willow House with nothing to do but watch the sun rise and the candles melt. He had been tasked to purchase a few day and evening gowns for Ms. Vernon and coach her on how to act in convincing the local parson and his wife she was Lady Analisa Hastings. It wasn't very difficult, but it was very boring.

"Relax, Teddy. All is going according to plan. Where is Ms. Vernon now?"

"She is napping. The final fittings were this afternoon and Her Ladyship's new wardrobe will be ready by midday tomorrow."

"Is her performance believable?"

"She'll do." Teddy poured himself a glass of brandy and offered one to Thomas. "If she keeps to simple responses and keeps her head down, no one will be the wiser."

"What of her signature?"

"She has been practicing every day. Her signature is almost identical to that of Lady Walsenburg. It may not fool a handwriting expert, but it will pass inspection for most."

"Marvelous! We are ready. We will arrive at Mariposa's parish chapel the day after tomorrow. We will be dusty, hungry, and in disarray but very much in love. Her Ladyship will be weak but adamant that we marry without delay. I will present the special license. The marriage will be officially recorded, and I will return beside my blushing bride as Mr. and Mrs. Thomas Smyth." He rose abruptly and patted Teddy hard on the back. "Now, let us order something to eat. I am starving."

CHAPTER THIRTEEN

"Relax, Ms. Vernon. Twenty minutes, in and out. Cough from time to time. Look adoringly into my eyes as often as possible and give monosyllabic responses as required."

"Are you confident with your signature?" Teddy went over the plan again and again in his head as he'd been doing for the past three days.

"If my hand doesn't shake too badly." She gave him a lopsided grin. "I will be fine, Teddy. I must admit I am a little nervous, but I will be fine."

The rented coach pulled up to the courtyard steps of the local parish chapel. Teddy jumped out first to survey the area. All good.

Thomas stepped out next, turning to assist the dowager marchioness, his betrothed, in alighting the coach.

She kept her delicate silk handkerchief at her lips, feigning a pending cough.

They walked up to the main chapel doors and entered, looking around for the parson. There were two older women seated midway up and to the left. Locals with too much time on their hands.

A young lady came rushing up to greet them. "Good day, sir, madam. How can I assist you this fine afternoon?"

"This lovely lady and I would like to be married. Immediately."

"Congratulations to you both. My father will be with you shortly. He has only just finished performing the nuptials for another happy couple. If you would be so kind as to wait here. I will be back for you both in a moment."

The pretty young lady disappeared into the back of the chapel.

"Shall we sit while we wait?" Miriam nodded and followed him to the closest pew. "Keep looking at me adoringly."

"There is no one here to witness. That would simply be a waste of a good performance."

"No detail is unnecessary, darling. You are aware of what you can see but you can only guess at what is hidden. From the moment we alighted the coach, you became Analisa Hastings, my adorable and lovesick blushing bride to be." He reached for her hand. "If we do not believe it, no one else will."

"Yes, my darling." She actually blushed. Perfect.

There were muffled sounds coming from the back of the chapel and moments later an older man and woman emerged. It must be the preacher and his wife come to escort them back to the chamber where the ceremony would take place.

"Good day, sir, madam; I understand you are here to be joined in matrimony. How wonderful."

Thomas smiled lovingly at his wife to be. "I still cannot believe she accepted my suit." He extended his hand to her for her to rise and join him.

She did so while keeping her eyes fixed on him and gave a little cough into her handkerchief for good measure.

"We have had a long and challenging journey. My lady is exhausted." He turned to her. "If you would rather wait a few days until you have recovered, my dear, we could postpone the nuptials."

On cue she stepped closer to him. "Not a day. I love you."

The parson and his wife smiled at each other. "How lovely. If you will both follow us. It will take us a few minutes to set up for the ceremony. The young lady can rest with a cup of tea and a few freshly baked biscuits. They are just out of the oven. This is my husband; the Reverend Samuel Thatcher. I am Eunice Thatcher." She turned to her right. "This is our youngest daughter, Bess. She will be a witness for the ceremony unless you have brought witnesses of your own."

"We do have one witness with us, but we would welcome and appreciate Bess's participation. Thank you."

The group now proceeded to a small chamber in the back of the main chapel. It had a small altar, two pews and two kneelers. There was a pianoforte in the corner and a small table and two chairs in the back of the room. Fresh flowers had been arranged in a few strategic places throughout the room, and the mandatory candles were blazing on the altar.

The entire room's content appeared to be mobile and interchangeable. Thomas imagined it being transformed from a wedding to a baptism to a funeral with relative ease.

"Bess, my dear, would you please fetch the young lady a cup of tea and some biscuits?"

"Yes, Mama, right away."

Vivian, or rather Analisa, sat down and allowed Thomas to do all of the talking.

"I believe you will be requiring this." From his coat pocket he extracted the special license. "We intended to marry at home with our family and friends all around us, but the weather turned sour in the middle of our journey and our chaperone became ill. We left her with friends in Farthington and went on ahead. Unfortunately, arriving at home, alone and without a chaperone may put a stain on my lady's reputation, so we opted to marry before we returned."

"That is very considerate of you, sir. And quite the practical thing to do."

Bess returned with the refreshments while Mrs. Thatcher busied herself with setting the stage for the ceremony.

Minutes later all was in order. "Shall we begin?" the reverend announced as his wife and daughter joined him by the altar.

Thomas offered his intended his hand and they proceeded together to the front of the room to be married.

"Are we to wait for your witness?"

From the door, Teddy stepped in. "I am here, sir. My apologies for the delay."

"Not at all, my good man." The reverend turned back to the happy couple. "Now, may I have your names?"

The ceremony went off without a hitch. The register was signed. The fee was paid, and the couple was now husband and wife.

The hard part was done. Now came the battles and the fun.

CHAPTER FOURTEEN

A Hidden Island Manor in Sonastare

There was a knock on her sitting room door. "Enter."

Desdemona opened the door and curtsied. "Begging your pardon, my lady, Mr. Iago is here to see you."

Analisa rose and made her way to the main chamber.

"Mr. Iago. I hope you are here to tell me I am being released. It has been a week and my patience is running pathetically short."

"Good evening, my lady. I have indeed come to announce your release. If you will make yourself ready for departure at sunup, we should have you home by nightfall."

"It is about time. I assume the play is proceeding according to your script."

"All is as staged, my lady." He took a step toward her. "I want you to know how much we have all appreciated your amiability during these difficult times. I realize this has been a very uncomfortable ordeal for you."

"There is no need for gratitude, sir, as I was given very little recourse but to comply." She turned to leave. Without facing him she stated, "I hope I can still count on your word that no one has or will be hurt in the execution of this little performance."

"I stand by my word, my lady." After a slight pause he added, "I expect you will be quite cross with me when you are made fully aware of our intentions. I hope that even in your anger you will believe that if there had been any other way, we would not have put you in this position."

"And I hope you will understand I cannot forgive what I do not understand. That said, you and your staff have treated me well and for that courtesy, I am grateful." With that, she entered her sitting room and closed the door. She sat at her desk and let the tears come. As relieved as she was to be going home, there was fear and apprehension in what she would find when she arrived.

CHAPTER FIFTEEN

As promised, Mr. Iago was waiting for her in the main parlor of her prison when she exited her rooms. "Punctuality is an admirable characteristic in anyone, Mr. Iago. Are we prepared to depart?"

"At your convenience, my lady. I regret we will need to use the hood until we reach the point of handoff. I hope you will indulge us just once more."

"You make it sound as if it were a request rather than a requirement. We both know better." She closed her eyes awaiting the silk hood to be applied. She simultaneously extended her hands to be bound as they were when she was first abducted.

"The bindings will not be necessary, my lady, if you promise to behave yourself. It will not be a long journey." She lowered her arms to her side. Thank heavens for small favors.

The same small boat that had brought them to the island brought them back on shore. From boat to coach and onward to freedom.

"Do I have your permission to remove the hood, Mr. Iago?"

"Certainly, my lady. Unfortunately, I cannot offer you a view. I hope this will not be too much of an inconvenience."

"Relative to these past few days, it is no inconvenience at all, sir."

An hour later they were coming to a stop. "Have we arrived at our final destination?"

"We will be making a transition here before the final leg of your journey home."

"I will need to don the hood once more, yes?"

"If you would be so kind, my lady."

She placed the hood on her own head and heard the coach door open. Mr. Iago carefully led her out of the coach and protectively guided her inside the building where they were to make the transition.

"You may remove the hood now, my lady."

As she did so, a familiar face came into focus. "Mr. Smyth! Thank heavens you are well. You were not with us when we arrived on the island, and Mr. Iago refused to tell me what had become of you."

Thomas looked at Alexander. Alexander simply bowed and exited the room.

"Have you any idea what is going on? Are we being held for ransom?"

"I am fully aware of what is going on, my lady, and we are definitely not being held for ransom. Please have a seat and I will explain the situation to you."

A little frightened but curious, Analisa took a seat.

"First I would like to apologize for what you have been forced to endure these past few days. Unfortunately, I had no other choice. I hope to someday have your understanding if not your forgiveness."

"Mr. Smyth, you are frightening me. Do you confess to being the mastermind behind this drama?"

"I am indeed, my lady."

She shot to her feet. "How? Why? Who are you? What do you want of me? Of us?"

"If you will resume your seat, my lady, I will do my best to explain."

She sat back down slowly. Desdemona entered the room with a tray of coffee, tea, assorted fruits, and some light pastries.

"I know you have not broken your fast but under the circumstances, I did not feel your stomach would appreciate a heavy meal."

"An astute observation, Mr. Smyth. I find I have lost what little appetite I had. Please go on with your explanation."

"You may or may not be aware of much of what I am about to share. So I will start from where I consider is a relevant beginning.

"Are you familiar with the Barony of Pennington?" Analisa shook her head. "It is a relatively obscure barony in the kingdom of Artemisia. When the twelfth Baron of Pennington died some twelve years past, without issue, the Artemisian parliament traced his closest living heir to Sonastare. Your mother, my lady."

"My mother hailed from Artemisia? I had not known. Not that it would have mattered. My family never allied itself with any resentment toward Artemisia. Why would she not share this information with the family?"

"She may not have known herself. Her line extends back three generations as Sonastare citizens. Regardless, Artemisian officials reached out to your parents. Eleven years ago, your mother assumed the title thirteenth Baroness Pennington with all entailed and unentailed lands and privileges."

Analisa's head was spinning. "Please give me a moment to process this information, Mr. Smyth." She stood and began to pace. She thought back through her childhood for any clues that her parents were aware of this association. There was nothing. Not a story, not even a fairy tale of how her mother's family immigrated to Sonastare. She sat back down. "Please go on, sir."

"Your mother had little interest in the barony with the exception of making sure its tenants and retainers were protected and provided for.

"Your father, however, saw it as an opportunity. He had worried for years that without a male heir, you and your mother would be left to the mercies of your cousin the current Duke of Colton. You had long since married and he was confident your husband, the marquess, would provide for you and your children, but your mother was still vulnerable.

"He began making investments in and through the barony as a contingency plan. I do not believe his intention was to amass a fortune, but simply to leave your mother with enough to keep her in the comfort and style she had become accustomed to under his care."

"My father was an astute businessman and valued his family above all else. I am not surprised by his tactics. But why was I not informed?"

"I believe the plan's greatest asset was its anonymity. Your father never took any capital from the barony's portfolio. Capital only entered and profits were immediately reinvested.

"Your father also had the foresight of retaining Mr. Miles Granger as his man of business for the barony. Mr. Granger is not only staunchly loyal and discreet, but he is also one of the savviest investors in the two kingdoms.

"The late duke gave Granger full authority over the barony. His instructions were simple; look after the people associated with the barony, invest wisely and aggressively, keep the barony above reproach, and limit communications to two scheduled gatherings each year other than emergencies. Mr. Granger is the best. So good, that today no one is wise to the fact that you, my lady, are the current and fourteenth Baroness of Pennington."

"I am what? How can this be? I have not been contacted. This cannot be official or legal."

"I can assure you; it is all official and completely legal.

"Now for the more nefarious part of this story. I am certain you can deduce that if you are not yet aware of these circumstances, neither is the world. This will not be the case for very much longer.

"Once your actual circumstances are revealed, you will be placed in a uniquely vulnerable position. My aim is to protect you from the fallout."

"And just how do you intend to do that, Mr. Smyth?"

"Done, my lady. As of three days ago, we became man and wife."

All she could do was stare in disbelief. Was he mad? That was the only explanation for all of this. Relatives hailing from Artemisia, baroness, married? This was all nonsense. The man had gone insane.

Thomas smiled at her. "This is neither madness nor nonsense. I can assure you it is all the truth. And although we did marry by proxy, we are married." He presented her with the marriage license. Her signature next to his confirmed the union.

"I have never heard of a marriage by proxy, sir. This cannot be legal."

"Legal and binding, my lady. But I do require your cooperation to have it accepted by society at large."

"And just why, in heaven's name, would I cooperate with this shameful and disgraceful deception?"

"Let me convince you how it may be in your best interest to play along. Would you give me your word to listen with an open mind and heart?"

She wanted to walk up and slap the man senseless. "Why should I listen to anything you have to say?"

"For one thing, you have nothing to lose and much to gain. Even if you refuse to participate, untangling this web will not be simple, cheap, or quick. I can keep this tied up for decades in two kingdoms. Do you really want to go through that or put your family through it? What of your reputation? Your family name? Collateral damage to your friends and to society?"

"Claudius. That is who you remind me of."

"I beg your pardon, my lady."

"The first request made of me when recently abducted was to give my jailer a name. Since he would not give me his true identity, he requested I name him. The first name that came to mind was Iago. The villain in Shakespeare's *Othello*. It is only appropriate I name you Claudius. Are you familiar with Hamlet, Mr. Smyth?"

"I am indeed, my lady. I will not argue the name is well deserved. If it pleases you to baptize me as such, I will humbly accept. For you and you alone from this day forward I will answer to Claudius. May I be permitted to continue, my lady?"

She waved her hand in royal fashion.

"You will not dispute the marriage but promote the union as legitimate if not happy. We will live as husband and wife for an undetermined period of time until we both agree to dissolve the marriage. During this time, you will not be expected to perform any wifely duties relative to sexual activities. That is, unless you request the attention; then I would be more than happy to oblige you as a good and dutiful husband."

"You may relieve yourself of any expectations and illusions you may be holding on that subject, sir. I do not find villains particularly attractive."

"As you wish, my lady." He gave her a mocking but respectful nod. "As your husband, beloved or not, I will have final say on all matters related to the barony and an equal say in financial matters relating to your widow's pension, properties, and assets.

"At the dissolution of our marriage, you will award me a very generous settlement and we will part ways amicably.

"Although you have leave to argue with me in private, you will never contradict or disagree with my decisions openly. Do we have an accord?"

This was not happening. Not to her. She had been a good person her entire life. She'd never taken from or mistreated anyone. She showered her family and her children with love and support. Then why did she find herself in this untenable position? And where was her son during all this? Surely he was frantic with worry. He must have the entire kingdom out looking for her.

She was the daughter of a duke and the widow and mother of a marquess. These were powerful positions. There must be a solution.

A way out of this situation with minimal damage to all concerned. She simply had to be patient.

"It seems you have placed me in a very difficult position, Lord Claudius. I apparently have little choice in the matter. But I promise you this. I will be vigilant. If I find the slightest chink in your malicious armor, I will exploit it in my own defense. Mark my words and watch your back, sir."

"I would expect nothing less from an adversary as formidable as yourself, my lady. One more thing. As distasteful as it may be, I must be allowed to use your given name from this point forward. It would not do for a husband to address his wife by her title in private."

"You have taken everything else from me, sir. Why not my title as well. You may call me Analisa but never Ana. That privilege is reserved for those I love and those who love me."

"One final detail. How I rescued you."

"Rescued me? How dare you."

"My dear Analisa. It is an important feature of this drama. We will logically be asked what happened and how we came to be together and married."

Could this get more complicated? Again, all she did was wave her hand to proceed.

"You were groggy when I found you in a small boat shed just outside the town of Mariposa. Your captors kept you drugged, so you do not remember much about your ordeal. All you recall is being abducted in the museum gardens and nothing else until I found and rescued you. You were so grateful you fell desperately in love with me, as I did with you, and we married in Mariposa yesterday morning before returning to Salassio. I will fill in the details of my heroic search for you. It will be quite dramatic. You may even shed a few tears at my recollection."

"Mr. Smyth, no one will believe that wild story. It is preposterous. A ten-year-old girl would not be so naïve or so reckless."

"There is the brilliance of this plan. It does not need to be believed; it must simply be accepted as true. I will make sure the facts support the story."

He stood and walked over to her, extending his hand. "I believe this belongs to you." In his palm he held her emerald ring. She aggressively snatched it up as if afraid he would decide to keep it after all. "We are now ready to resume our journey to Salassio and Bellstrand." She accepted his assistance to stand. He tucked her hand in the crook of his arm and waved toward the door. "Shall we, Analisa?"

Without a single word, they walked outside, where a leased coach awaited to transport them home.

This was a nightmare. An absolute and unequivocal nightmare. *Please, Lord, allow me to awaken before I expire in anguish.*

CHAPTER SIXTEEN

The Kelt Residence, Bellstrand Island, Sonastare

"Pardon my interruption, my lady, but I am certain you would want to know immediately. The Dowager Marchioness of Walsenburg has returned," Summers, Lady Kelt's butler, announced as he entered the informal parlor.

Lady Kelt was having a late afternoon tea with the Duchess of Welby and almost let her teacup fall out of her grasp at the news.

"Oh thank the good Lord. Any news of her condition? Is she hurt or ill?"

"Nothing further, my lady. She is being escorted over by Collinsworth on the royal ferry."

"Has Walsenburg been notified?"

"He has, my lady. He and the marchioness are said to be on their way to the pier to await the lady's arrival."

"Thank you, Summers." She turned to her maid. "Please bring me my shawl and have the coach made ready immediately. We are off to the pier."

"Will you join me, Ada?"

The duchess was already walking toward the door. "As if you could stop me. This is one instance I wish women were permitted to ride astride. We could get there in half the time."

"You, my dear, are the Duchess of Welby. You could ride a goat astride and no one would raise an eyebrow."

"Maybe the goat."

They were both laughing hysterically as they boarded Lady Kelt's coach. Much of their merriment was relief, but some was nervous tension at the fear of finding Analisa hurt. They had all heard stories of the horrible things that happened to women who were abducted. The odds were not in their favor but at least they had their friend back. They would deal with whatever fallout was presented to them.

The pier was relatively empty when they arrived. The royal ferry was meant for the exclusive use of the royal family and their guests. It had its own private and secure dock assigned to it. It had also been placed at the disposal of Bellstrand's authorities during this emergency.

The ferry was just docking when Lady Kelt's carriage arrived. Both ladies alighted the coach and hurried into the private royal pier pavilion. They quickly found Lady Cross and the Marques and Marchioness of Walsenburg anxiously waiting for Analisa to disembark.

They watched as she came forward accompanied by Collinsworth and five other gentlemen. Four were dressed in military garb, clearly identifying them as officers in Bellstrand's security forces, but at her side was Thomas Smyth. This was an odd turn of events. Everyone looked quite confused as Analisa had her arm intertwined with Mr. Smyth's. Was she ill? Was he assisting her due to a lack of strength on her part?

Collinsworth led the group as they approached the family. "My lord, my ladies; I will leave Mrs. Smyth in your capable hands." He then turned to Analisa with a bow. "I am very grateful you have been returned to us safely, madam. We may have a few more questions for you in the coming days in order to close our report. We will reach out to you at Miramarea Abbey if you have no objections."

"None at all, Mr. Collinsworth. And thank you and your men very much for handling this situation so smoothly."

The escort withdrew, leaving them alone with the welcoming family and friends.

"Mrs. Smyth?" George was visibly both confused and upset. "What in the world happened to you this week, Mother?"

"This is not the time, Walsenburg," the duchess interrupted. "We need to get her home and fed. She looks as if she has lost a stone's weight if not more."

"Yes of course, Your Grace. My apologies, Mother. My coach is just outside. We will take you back to Miramarea Abbey, where we can care for you properly."

The ride back to the Walsenburg estate was short but tense. Thomas held on tightly to Analisa. He was every inch the considerate, worried, and doting husband.

Once inside Miramarea, everyone adjourned to the more informal second level. The family floor as they referred to it.

Miramarea Abbey was one of the most luxurious estates on Bellstrand, boasting more than two hundred rooms with eighty guest quarters including more lavish and private guest houses close to the main house but separate. Each guest house had accommodations for a personal staff of retainers and a small, private kitchen and dining room for very private parties and entertainment.

The main house had three floors not counting servant's quarters; the kitchen and other utilities were located in the basement. The ground floor or first level was all formal living for official functions and important events. The dining table easily sat one hundred and sixty guests. The main of four ballrooms accommodated countless guests and three alcoves for three separate orchestras to play at once. The library was extensive with every important first edition tome cataloged. There were even provisions for establishing retiring rooms for women and men if required with every comfort and luxury available for the time.

On the second level, you would find the family quarters. The entire floor was designed for family privacy and comfort. There were twelve bedrooms with the lord's and lady's bedchambers located at the end of the east wing, designed to provide the master and mistress of the house with the most advantageous view of the main gardens, taking best advantage of the morning sun. A formal and informal dining room. A master and a mistress study. A smaller library than the one found on the ground floor and, of course, the family salon.

It was here that all eyes turned to the newlyweds.

"First and most importantly. Are you hurt, Analisa? Have you suffered any illness or ill-treatment while in the ruffians' hands?" Maggie was looking Analisa up and down.

"Nothing other than the weight loss and some associated weakness." She looked at Thomas. "As I told Mr. Collinsworth, I really do not remember much after I was abducted. I believe they had me drugged the entire time."

"Oh, my dear. You do not think they did anything untoward, do you? We have all read terrible stories of women being taken and cruelly abused by their captors." Lady Kelt was horrified at her own thoughts.

"No, no; nothing of the kind. I believe something worse may have happened if Thomas had not come to my rescue." She almost choked on the words. "Thank heavens for Mr. Smyth."

All eyes turned to Thomas. "How did you find her, sir?" George was giving Thomas a dubious stare.

"Purely by luck and God's good grace." He sounded so confident, Analisa could almost believe him. She knew better of course.

"I initially followed one of the reports that Analisa was seen in a coach on the road to Mariposa. They described her as traveling in a plain black coach. Something told me this was the lead to investigate. At Hedgestone I was fortunate enough to find a fisherman who had seen a woman who fit Analisa's description being taken to an abandoned cabin by the cove."

84

He looked adoringly at Analisa. "I found her there. Groggy but safe. I took her to the safest inn at Mariposa and went in search of her abductors, but they must have realized Analisa had been rescued and left for parts unknown. No one seemed to know what direction they took, or I would have had the authorities engaged in a pursuit." He squeezed her hand. "I am just sorry I did not get my hands on those monsters."

A bit ambiguous but just enough information to make it believable. He was good, she would have to admit. Now came the unbelievable fairy tale. She knew someone would ask the obvious. Surprisingly, it was her daughter-in-law who voiced the question.

"That is quite an amazing tale, Mr. Smyth. We are all so very grateful you acted so decisively and were so very fortunate in your search." Was that an eye roll? Analisa knew most of those present were trying to decide how much of this story to believe. These were not simple-minded individuals. "But tell me, how did you go from rescuer to husband? That seems an extraordinary leap. Grateful as my mother-in-law may be, to marry her rescuer only hours after such an ordeal is difficult to conceive." Everyone held their breath with all eyes fixed on Thomas.

"Our tenderness for one another was not Cupid's instant arrow, my lady. I have had the pleasure of sharing Analisa's company at a number of occasions since I arrived in Sonastare. I will admit to you now I have been slowly falling in love with this exceptional lady a little more each time we met. The situation only seemed to intensify my affection. I could not bear anything happening to her. Imagine my surprise when I discovered she had similar feelings for me. We knew our relationship had grown too strong too quickly and that there would be many well-meaning and very well-founded objections to our association, but we could not deny our love." Thomas brought his forehead up against Analisa's.

His actions confused her. On an obvious level, she was uncomfortable with the display of affection. She had been brought up to reject any sign of public intimacy maternal or romantic.

85

Yet there was a part of her, on a primal level, that relished the affection. He was gentle and sweet. When he said her name, it was like a whispered prayer. Was any of what he confessed he felt genuine? Claudius! The man was a villain and a thief. None of this drivel was real. Not one single word of it.

"I impulsively asked for her hand and she mercifully accepted. We knew that waiting until our return to the bosom of our families to marry would likely present nothing but obstacles to our union. The last thing we needed was more to deal with. We married in Mariposa yesterday morning. And have not had a moment's regret since."

She was almost expecting "and they lived happily ever after" as a finale but his ending was good too.

"How very romantic. It is like a fairy tale, would you not say?" Lady Kelt was gushing. Not that she actually believed this absurd account. She simply wanted to refocus on Analisa. She looked tired and upset. She needed food and rest. "Well, my dear. We will leave you in the loving care of your son and his wife. George, please make certain she eats something before retiring even if she refuses." To Thomas she said, "Welcome to our little family Mr. Smyth. Take a couple of days to recuperate but I insist you come to my home for dinner in a week's time. I want to hear all the romantic details you have left out." She gave Joseline a quick curtsy. "Come along, Maggie, my dear. We must let them rest and reenergize."

They all rose. Maggie hugged Analisa and whispered, "If he is holding you against your will, squeeze my hand."

"God did not bless me with a sister, until you." Analisa kissed her cheeks. "All is well. We will talk more later."

CHAPTER SEVENTEEN

"I heard the dowager marchioness has returned safe and sound." Reardon Tenison did not look happy but was always in control. "You have less than one week to make good on your commitment to me, my lord. I hope you have a backup plan."

George didn't look at him. He was transfixed with the ivy growing just outside the window. Folton's was quiet this afternoon. With the exception of two other parties enjoying the day away from the responsibilities of the aristocracy, only the marquess and Lord Tenison were present.

"I understand your ship has not yet been released. No ship, no goods. No goods, no way of meeting your financial obligations." Tenison sat back in his chair. "Those two hundred and forty thousand acres are as good as mine."

"Much can happen in a week's time."

"Much was expected to happen this past week and did not." Tenison gave George a moment to relive his failed attempt at siphoning capital from his mother's coffers during her absence. "You had a once-in-a-lifetime opportunity and muffed it up. You could have had full control of the dowager's resources and you let it slip through your fingers. A pathetic failure."

George turned abruptly and stood ready to challenge the insult decisively.

Tenison raised his hands defensively. "I refer to the scheme, my lord. No insult intended."

The insult was not only intended but blatantly obvious to George. Discretion was the better part of valor. This man still held devastating cards over his head. No need in making a bad situation worse.

"I have no doubt you would have had little hesitation in having your own mother killed if it would improve your situation. Fortunately, we are not all as black-hearted as you," George replied.

"Fortunately, my mother was kind enough to leave this mortal coil on her own terms. She reached her limits as Lady Elena Grimm-Tenison, Viscountess Abernathy, and abruptly abdicated her position with the apothecary's assistance." Tenison smirked. "I would never have hurt her. She brought nothing to the title but a pretty face."

"Fortunately for her."

"Now, Lady Analisa Elizabeth Childress-Hastings, Dowager Marchioness of Walsenburg, is an entirely different story. Class, beauty, impressive lineage, enviable connections, and a huge fortune thanks to her father and yours, my lord." Tenison folded his hands across his chest. "It is enough to tempt anyone."

George turned away. He could barely stomach this miscreant.

Tenison wasn't done digging in the knife. "Rumor has it, Lady Analisa Elizabeth Childress-Hastings is now Mrs. Analisa Smyth of nowhere. How long before she will be forced to vacate her Bellstrand home? There is a standard to maintain."

"You look after your family and leave me to look after mine." George turned to look straight into Tenison's eyes. "Oh right. You have no family to look after. Rumor has it, your wife despises you as much as everyone else who knows you. Two years and no heir. It must be devastating for you, Tenison. But I would not worry over much. At the rate the current Viscountess Abernathy is taking on lovers, I would not be surprised if she were not already with child. Not your child, of course, but any blood is an improvement over yours."

Tenison stood. "Five days, Walsenburg. Not a minute longer." He exited the room and the club, for parts unknown.

CHAPTER EIGHTEEN

They'd been assigned the largest of the estate cottages as their temporary lodgings. George had initially insisted they stay in the main house. Analisa had convinced him that having the current and former mistresses of the house underfoot would be overly confusing for the staff. The cottage was close to the main house but would offer the newlyweds privacy. Not too reluctantly, George acquiesced.

It may have been called a cottage, but it was anything but modest. With five sleeping quarters, Analisa and Thomas each had their own bedroom as well as private sitting rooms. There was a morning room, study, formal and informal dining rooms, and a modest receiving room for guests.

"George will have your entire story investigated, you know." Breakfast and the midday meal had been catered by the main kitchens. Analisa had sent for Mrs. Hortense Parker, Georgette, and Tully to attend her while at Miramarea Abbey. Until they arrived, the couple would rely on her son's hospitality.

Her correspondence had been brought over from Serenity Hall, the dowager house. She was going through each missive carefully.

Thomas had received several documents himself delivered by a very severe and extremely quiet messenger. He was not paying attention. "Pardon me, my dear. I did not hear you."

"I was simply commenting that the story you told last evening will be scrutinized. Both George and Maggie will send inquiries to confirm every detail of our ordeal. You will be found out and this entire nightmare will be put to rest once and for all."

He looked at her over the document he was currently scanning. A devilish grin that seemed to light up his entire face took hold. He really was the most beautiful man she had ever seen. "My dear. Do you not think that I have anticipated an investigation? I have planned for this inevitability. Every possible contingency has been taken into account. Do you not have any faith in me?" He could not help but tease her a little bit, as he was enjoying himself, and everything was proceeding according to plan.

Claudius! He is *Claudius.* "I barely know you, sir. Besides, my faith in you was not a condition of our agreement."

"Correct as always, my darling." He gathered his documents. "I will prepare for dinner. The marchioness has requested our presence at table this evening." He gave her an elaborate and official bow. He was whistling as he withdrew to his suite.

A footman had been temporarily assigned to act as Thomas's valet. Bruce was in his mid-twenties, strong, and ambitious. He saw this as a great opportunity to elevate his status. "I have had the bathing drum brought in, and the water is being heated now, my lord."

Thomas regarded Bruce with compassion but felt compelled to correct him for his own sake. "You are Bruce, correct?" The young man nodded. "Well, Bruce, if you are going to be successful as a retainer, particularly a valet, you must pay close attention to courtesies, customs, and propriety. First, the euphemism for that large bucket where I will wash is a *bathtub*. Referring to anything your master or mistress is associated with, with anything other than an air of loftiness will be considered an insult.

"Secondly, I am untitled. The only appropriate addresses for me are sir or mister. Slips like those in the presence of your master may have you sacked."

"Yes my...sir. Thank you for correcting me. I do want to do a good job for you, sir."

"Of that I have no doubt. You help me, and I will help you. A partnership of sorts." Thomas began to undress, anticipating the water was ready for him in his sitting room, which would serve as a bathing room this evening.

"I would keep an eye on innovations on the horizon. I have been told of modern homes having indoor plumbing these days."

"Indoor what, sir?"

"Indoor plumbing. Water is guided to a final destination through a series of pipes. This will make the toting of water up and down stairs obsolete. Research the technology for the marquess. He will appreciate your initiative."

"Thank you, sir. I will certainly do that." Bruce liked this Mr. Smyth regardless of the rumors. He was certainly more human than the marquess or his wife. If he did a good job, maybe Mr. Smyth would offer him a permanent position as his valet when he and Mrs. Smyth retired to their own home.

CHAPTER NINETEEN

Thomas did not realize how in need of relaxation he was. The warm water was very soothing and the feeling of being clean was equally welcomed. He heard the door to his sitting room open. He assumed it was Bruce come to dry him off and help him dress for dinner. He had been soaking for a while. The water was beginning to cool but was still warm enough to be enjoyed. He stood, allowing the water to drain off his body while he waited for Bruce to apply the drying cloth. He stood there for what seemed like minutes.

"Please forgive me, I must have entered the wrong chamber."

Thomas turned at the sound of a female voice. Not just any female but his wife. "No apologies necessary, my dear. I am your husband. There is no room in my home where you do not have free access." He stood there facing her as bare as he had come into this world. He gave her a moment. "Were you looking for me?"

"Yes, I did not realize you would be utilizing the sitting room as a bathing chamber."

"Where do you bathe?"

"I have the bathing tub brought to my bedchamber. It is more convenient for the servants as the door is wider."

"I had not considered that. I will bathe in my chamber in the future. Thank you for bringing this to my attention."

She had not taken her eyes from his body since she entered. A widow married many years, the sight of a naked man did not surprise or upset her. Since she continued to stare without moving, he thought he'd press his advantage.

"The water is still warm. I could have Bruce bring up more hot water if you would care to join me."

"That would not be necessary nor appropriate."

"What could be more appropriate than a wife sharing a bath with her husband?" He held out his hand inviting her to join him. "It would save the servants the effort of duplicating this process for you later in your chamber, no?"

Her mind seemed to reengage. "You are the most beautiful man I have ever seen, Mr. Smyth. I am a mature woman. I have known love and even lust. I have enjoyed the delights of the flesh, but I have never been treated as a plaything or a pawn on a chessboard.

"You wish to tempt me into a compromising position, further entangling this web you weave so methodically, but you will fail. I may have been raised a lady but do not make the mistake of believing I was not born a woman first." She turned to leave. "When it comes to carnal games, sir, never underestimate a woman. We hold the power and, once educated, we make most of the decisions. But our greatest gift is allowing men to believe they are in control. Foolish.

"I came to tell you; a satchel has arrived for you by special courier. I was informed it was urgent and required your immediate attention. The courier awaits in the receiving room." She walked out, closing the door gently behind her.

A few moments later Bruce came in. "Are you ready to dress for dinner, sir?"

Thomas laughed out loud. "Very well done, Bruce. Pretending you do not know what went on here just moments ago and completely ignoring my state of arousal. Now, those are excellent traits in a competent retainer. I have a feeling you will make an exceptional valet someday."

"If you say so, sir."

Thomas dressed and hurried to meet with the courier. He found him standing by the window as he entered the small but elegant receiving room. The courier turned and bowed.

"I am not deserving of those courtesies, sir. I am a mister, not a lord," Thomas admonished gently and without rancor.

The young man looked confused but quickly righted himself. He walked over to Thomas and extended the satchel he carried. "I was told to present this to you and you alone, sir."

Thomas took and opened the satchel. He scanned the first few pages. "Thank you. There will be no response."

The young courier gave him a slight nod and took his leave. As he made his way to the front door, he passed by Analisa standing in the hall just outside the receiving room.

The courier stopped, looking from Thomas to Analisa for a moment. He bowed to her before he left the cottage.

Something strange had just occurred to her. How could Thomas have couriers freely enter and leave Bellstrand? Entry was by invitation only, and she had not extended any such invitations or permissions. Had Thomas made this request of George? Why would he not come to her? Was there a conspiracy afoot? She'd speak with George after dinner this evening.

CHAPTER TWENTY

They walked side by side to the main house through the adjacent, formal blossom gardens. They entered the house through the French doors in the main ballroom and were immediately greeted by Dobbs, the marquess's butler.

"Good evening, Mr. Smyth, Mrs. Smyth." He stepped aside to allow them entry. "Would you follow me up to the family dining room?"

Analisa had been mistress of this house for over twenty years. If anyone knew where the family dining room was located, it would certainly be the former mistress of the house. Sometimes she really hated the useless protocols of the nobility.

"Thank you, Dobbs." They fell in line behind the butler.

They arrived to find George and Joseline already at table. George immediately stood as she entered.

"Good evening, Mother." He came closer, arms outstretched. He bussed her cheeks. Turning half a shoulder in his direction, he said, "Mr. Smyth. So happy you could join us this evening."

"How could we refuse such a gracious invitation from the marchioness." Thomas knew the invitation was extended out of a sense of obligation and duty rather than genuine affection.

Joseline never rose. The group approached the table with some underlying discomfort. "Joseline, you are looking lovely this evening. That color brings out the beautiful brilliance of your eyes." Analisa had always found Joseline a beautiful woman, but the severity of her personality served to tarnish that beauty somehow. But there was something about her this evening. Her face was fuller. More lovely.

They all sat and Joseline signaled for the first course to be served.

"I hope you both had a restful night after your chaotic experience." Joseline was looking at George as she made the comment. This was not going to be relaxing or fun.

Dinner proceeded, tense but without incident. They concentrated on discussing upcoming plans. What social events they would attend. Meetings with solicitors and government officials and mundane day-to-day logistics.

"Do you know where you will be living?" Joseline asked of no one in particular. All eyes focused on her. "I meant no disrespect; I simply raised a logical question. As a former member of Sonastare's nobility, you will no longer be able to reside on Bellstrand as Mr. and Mrs. Smyth."

Analisa was taken aback. Not by the fact that she would need to relocate. She knew this to be one of the inflexible standards of Bellstrand residency. She had several properties and estates throughout Sonastare where she could go. Both her late husband and late father had seen to that. She was astonished Joseline would be so crude as to voice the obvious yet painful truth with seemingly no regard for Analisa's feelings.

And then, like a bolt of lightning, it struck her. Joseline felt jealousy for Analisa. At least for her rank and position. They were both the daughters of dukes with impeccable lineage. But where Analisa was gregarious, altruistic, and approachable, Joseline was reserved and unsociable. She was not a bad person; she simply didn't know how to be, well, benevolent. Analisa would not be angry or hurt. She didn't believe Joseline meant to be cruel.

In an effort to lessen the negative impact of her daughter-in-law's inappropriate comment, Analisa laughed off the entire matter. "Come now. We are among family, are we not? If you cannot speak frankly with your own kin, we should not consider ourselves intimates."

Thomas and she exchanged a look of "well done." She adjusted her napkin as a momentary pause to collect her thoughts. Assuming Thomas would step in to take over the conversation, she kept silent, and when he did not come forward, she continued.

"Thomas and I have discussed the situation and our alternatives. The estate at Bellmorrow would be our best option. It is an active parish and the main house is fully staffed if only at a bare minimum. I would bring Serenity Hall's staff, those who wish to join us." She looked around the table for reactions. "What do you think, Thomas?"

Her question was more asking his feedback to her addressing the issue rather than his thoughts on the Bellmorrow option. "I think it a perfect solution, my dear." He winked at her. Cheeky fellow.

"The matter is settled then. We will send word to Bellmorrow and to Serenity Hall first thing tomorrow morning to begin preparations."

Joseline saw an opportunity. "If you have no objections, George, we could make use of the property as my parents' home on the island. Sadly, the duchy does not currently have a residence here and I know they would dearly love being closer to us now that we are expecting."

George looked at his mother and had the good graces to blush at his wife's lack of tact. Moreover, George knew that Joseline's plans were impossible.

This was not the time for censure. And all Analisa now cared about was that she would soon become a grandmother.

"Oh, my dear! How wonderful. You are increasing. I am going to be a grandmother. I could not be happier. When is the baby due?"

"In early winter, I believe." Joseline was caught a little off guard. The baby wasn't important. It was her duty to give the marquisate an heir. What mattered was social standing and that meant the dowager house. "So, you would not be hurt if we repurposed Serenity Hall?"

George stepped in. "I am afraid that is not possible, Joseline. Serenity Hall is not an asset of the marquisate. It was a personal gift to my mother from my father on their twentieth anniversary."

"Then we will purchase it from her. It would meet our needs perfectly and she cannot possibly want a property she cannot use."

Analisa was saddened by Joseline's one dimensional thinking but she had always made allowances for youth. "The Duke and Duchess of Dials are, of course, always welcome to use Serenity Hall whenever and for as long as they desire, my dear. As I said, we are family."

This did not please Joseline. There had to be a law forbidding untitled nobles from owning property on Bellstrand.

The party moved to the family rooms and all Analisa wanted to talk about was her soon-to-be grandchild.

CHAPTER TWENTY-ONE

"I received word this afternoon from Tenison, my lord. He tells me your time has expired. He expects and demands the deed to the Gables acreage by sunset tomorrow." Daniel Crossings delivered the bad news. The *Prospero* had not made port, and Tenison wanted his forfeiture.

The loss of this valuable property would be a significant financial blow to the marquisate. There was considerable rents and revenue to be gathered from this land. George knew this could set him up for ultimate ruin. He would have to sign over the property, but he was expecting Trenton to finance half the amount of the forfeiture. They were equal partners after all.

"Tell Tenison I will have a courier deliver the deed by midday tomorrow." He pulled some folded papers from his coat and handed them to Daniel. "I need for you to verify the facts of my mother's whirlwind marriage. I have written every detail down for you. Send whomever you need to verify the particulars. I need to know how I can terminate this ill-advised union and quickly."

Daniel tentatively scanned the papers and placed them in the inside pocket of his coat. "I will inform Viscount Abernathy to expect your courier by noon tomorrow." He patted his coat where the documents now rested. "And I will investigate this situation. Give me a few days. It should not take long." He hopped out of the coach and disappeared into the shadows.

CHAPTER TWENTY-TWO

"I would like to visit Artemisia and Pennington. I realize the details surrounding my inheritance are not yet public knowledge, but I have responsibilities to the title and to its people." Analisa wasn't sure if Thomas would agree but she felt compelled to make the attempt.

Since she discovered the consequences of her lineage, she felt uncertain of everything. Who she was. What she was. How much of what Thomas had told her was the truth? Was all of this simply more lies and subterfuge in his attempt to achieve his end? Whatever that was.

Thomas looked at her for a long time. "Bellmorrow borders Artemisia to the west, does it not?"

"It does. The river Mara separates the kingdoms. My father once told me the story of how the fifth Duke of Colton made a heroic stand on the shores of the Mara defending our king. The land was bestowed on Colton in appreciation of his leadership and self-sacrifice. Although the property is not entailed, it has never been sold as it was part of the ducal inheritance. Until recently that is, when my late husband took possession of Bellmorrow. I am not sure when or why this happened. I have always assumed Bellmorrow was part of my dowry."

"What would you say to our taking up residence at The Cloisters in Bellmorrow immediately?" He reached for a stack of documents on the desk to his right. He quickly scanned them and looked up at her with a grin.

"How do you know of The Cloisters?" She took two steps closer to his desk. "I have never shared the name with anyone."

"My dear. I am very good at what I do. Did you not think I have researched you, your family, and your entire life in minute detail?"

"Regardless of how good you are or may believe you are, Mr. Smyth, that name is not written down anywhere." She looked at him with such intensity he almost felt exposed for a moment. "The only explanation would be…"

There was a knock on the door. Thomas released the breath he didn't realize he'd been holding. "Enter."

Powers opened the door and took a step inside. "Pardon me, my lady, sir." He gave a slight bow and extended the salver containing a sealed letter. "This missive has just arrived for Her Ladyship from Bellmorrow. I thought you would want to see it right away."

Since Powers' arrival a few days ago, Analisa had been doing her best to remind him she no longer enjoyed a noble title. Powers refused to address her as anything but "my lady."

"Thank you, Powers." The butler withdrew as Analisa unsealed the note. She read it carefully twice. "It appears all is ready for our arrival in Bellmorrow. Or at least all will be by the time we arrive." She read part of it once more before continuing. "They also tell me they have seen strangers on the property who have not made their business known. They are concerned."

"How soon can you be ready to depart for Bellmorrow?" Thomas wanted to reach Bellmorrow as quickly as possible. He, too, had business in Artemisia that could not wait.

"I have already made arrangements to transport my personal items from Serenity Hall to Bellmorrow. I can be ready at daybreak."

"We leave at daybreak then." Thomas sat at his desk as if dismissing her.

"I will notify George and the others we will be leaving in the morning." She turned and quietly left the room.

CHAPTER TWENTY-THREE

It took them five days to reach Bellmorrow. With the exception of Tully and Bruce, who accompanied them, all other retainers and unnecessary luggage had been sent ahead.

Thomas had availed himself of his newly found wealth, purchasing an extensive wardrobe including a modern travel coach with four matching whites. Mr. and Mrs. Smyth traveled in style.

They'd been staying with friends and acquaintances of Analisa's along the way. Everyone seemed to roll out the red carpet for Analisa wherever she went. She and Thomas were given the best rooms their hosts had to offer. Resources, including servants, were made available to them without hesitation. Those who she had notified in advance had arranged elaborate dinner parties to welcome them to the family.

At just before sunset on the fifth day of travel, the new coach entered the main gates of the Bellmorrow estate. Two gatekeepers opened wide the front gates as soon as their identities were confirmed. The main house could not yet be seen but the grounds were immaculate.

Enormous oak trees lined the road leading up to the manor. To the left of the coach Thomas could see a body of water. It was too small to be a lake or a pond but too large to be a fountain. "These reflecting pools were designed for my great-grandfather in 1742 as a gift to his duchess commemorating the birth of his long-awaited heir. My grandfather the tenth Duke of Colton." She spoke with such pride. "Believing they were his to protect, my grandfather spared no expense in making them the envy of the kingdom. I will modernize the water distribution system.

"There are two maintenance crews on staff supporting the manor and all outlying buildings and structures. You will not find a faded door or a cracked pane of glass on the entire estate.

"We have year-round gardeners for both the public and the private gardens. A seasoned gamekeeper with a staff of thirty-five keep the forests stocked and the ponds teeming with fish.

"There is a private assembly hall on the grounds. It is designed for large, private balls and receptions given by the estate but we will open it to the city of Bellmorrow for use on occasion. It is notably larger and more impressive than the city's assembly hall."

None of it was expressed in a boastful manner. However, there was a great deal of pride in her description.

"It is a little-known fact that the Mara River bordering the entire east side of the property is part of the estate. Originally there was a fee for the use of the river. It generated significant revenues for the fifth Duke of Colton. We have long since suspended these fees as the Colton Duchy is not in need of the funds, and the people of both kingdoms are in need of the river."

The coach slowed and stopped under one of the more ornate porticos Thomas had ever seen. It had barely come to a complete stop when the door opened, and the step was lowered. A familiar face greeted them as he alighted the coach followed closely by Analisa.

"Powers. How lovely to see you again so soon." Analisa smiled at her longtime butler and friend.

"I trust my lady had a pleasant journey." Analisa didn't bother to correct his address any longer. She knew he'd be careful to address her as Mrs. Smyth in public but in private he refused to see her as anything but the noblewoman she was and would always be in his eyes.

"Most pleasant indeed. But exhausting as you can well imagine."

"Your rooms are all ready for you and Mr. Smyth, my lady." He proceeded into the house. "I had planned to assemble the entire house staff to greet you, but after your travels I thought it best to simply offer you a light meal and peaceful rest."

"You take such good care of me, Powers."

"That is why I am here, my lady. All you need do is relax. I will have all of your things brought in and put away before you know it."

Analisa turned to ascend the main stairwell followed by Tully and two housemaids.

Powers now addressed Thomas. "Mr. Smyth. Welcome to Bellmorrow. If you will follow Michael, he will bring you to your suites. I have arranged for a bath to be drawn for you, and a carafe of your preferred brandy is awaiting you. Cook has a light meal ready to be delivered at your request. If you would like something more substantial, please let Michael know."

"Thank you, Powers. Please notify the stable I will be riding out at dawn and to have my mount ready."

"Of course, sir."

Thomas ascended the staircase accompanied by Bruce following Michael the footman to what he was expecting to be a suite designed for the king himself.

They climbed to the second level, taking a right down the massive hall. Van Goghs, Delacroixs, and Repins lined the walls with a few tastefully placed Degas and Brancusis here and there.

They entered his suite of rooms at the end of the hall. Opening the solid oak double doors, they were greeted by a masculine, yet cozy living area done in dark hardwoods. An expansive wall of books adorned the inner wall, and a full bar, a love seat, and two very comfortable-looking wingback chairs surrounded a roaring fire.

Michael continued onto the next set of doors to the right of the library wall. Opening the doors wide he stepped aside, allowing Thomas to enter. There was an enormous four-poster bed made of dark mahogany, more books, and several pieces of furniture clearly designed for comfort. Everything was of the highest quality and most modern of tastes and design.

Michael indicated the door to their left. "This door is to your private study and sitting room, sir." He then walked over to the door at the opposite corner of the room. "This door leads to the sitting room you share with Mrs. Smyth. Is there anything else I can answer or fetch for you, sir?"

"No thank you, Michael. Please let Powers know he can serve in three-quarters of an hour after my bath."

"Very good, sir." Michael departed, closing the doors to the main suite entrance behind him, leaving Thomas and Bruce alone in the room.

"I assume you can find your way around?"

Bruce was looking a little overwhelmed but quickly recovered. "Of course, sir."

CHAPTER TWENTY-FOUR

Bellstrand Island, Sonastare

Dobbs came into the foyer to find a fashionable and determined gentleman pacing. "Good evening, sir. How may I be of service?"

Tenison presented a calling card. "Viscount Abernathy to see the marquess."

"Certainly, my lord. If you wait here a moment, I will see if His Lordship is in." Dobbs disappeared down the hall while Tenison returned to pacing.

The butler returned a few moments later. "If you will kindly follow me, my lord. Lord Walsenburg will receive you in his study."

The study door was open when they approached. Dobbs entered and announced the viscount and quickly took his leave.

"What the hell are you doing in my home, Tenison? We do not relate socially." George had turned over the deed to the Gables acreage over a week ago. He was hoping his association with Tenison was at an end. Why was this man in his home?

"Relax, my lord. All this stress cannot be good for your health." Without being invited to do so, Tenison took a seat and dared George to challenge him. George knew better.

"Our association concluded with my signing over the Gables acreage. I do not wish for any further association with you personally or professionally."

"Rest assured I am as unhappy about seeing you as you are of having me here, my lord." He relaxed back into his chair. "Unfortunately, we have a problem we must attend to right away. Once resolved, I will disappear from your life forever."

"What problem could we possibly share?"

"I had my man file for the deed in my name, and much to my surprise, the transfer was denied." He leaned forward with a vicious smile. "Now, you did not have anything to do with that, did you?"

"I do not know what you are talking about, Tenison. Now be gone from my presence. I have business I must attend to." He sat down and waved a dismissive hand, hoping the interloper would leave or disappear. He looked up to find Tenison standing, leaning on his white-knuckled fists, staring straight into his face.

"I have a schedule to keep, and taking ownership of the Gables acreage is a pivotal element in those plans. Use your considerable influence to find the problem and resolve it immediately, Walsenburg, or our next encounter will not be as pleasant."

"If this is some sort of delay or extortion tactic, Tenison, you are greatly mistaken. We have nothing further to discuss. Be gone." George was not good with confrontations. He could talk a good game and put on airs when necessary but if pushed too far he tended to crumble like a stale biscuit.

Tenison leaned in further, and George sat further back in his chair. "Immediately, do you hear me?" Tenison straightened up, adjusted his coat, gave George his back, and departed.

Dobbs came in looking very concerned. "Is everything all right, my lord? Viscount Abernathy left in quite a state."

"Everything is fine, Dobbs. I will need a footman to deliver a message right away."

On the mainland pier, less than a quarter mile from where the Bellstrand ferries docked, there were several public establishments known as The Promenade, where gentry and commoner alike would gather for a cool refreshment or a meal. You'd often see young folks gathered in casual conversations and families enjoying an evening by the water.

There were also a few pubs where men would congregate to discuss business and socialize. It was a well-known and respected strip, convenient when passage to Bellstrand was either delayed, denied, or inappropriate.

This was one of those occasions.

George disembarked *The Starling* and casually walked the quarter mile to the Emperor's Den pub.

Entering, he found only two other parties. Both seemed business related and completely oblivious of anything going on around them.

The pub was tastefully appointed. Clean with an air of respectability. Bar brawls and thievery were not tolerated in or around The Promenade. The Sonastare military saw to that.

"Good evening and welcome to the Emperor's Den. May I show you to a table, sir?" a young man greeted as he approached George. He was dressed in simple black and gray attire promoting uniformity. Keeping with the theme and respectability of the environment, ladies were not allowed to work in roles making direct contact with the public. They were welcomed behind the scenes as cooks and launderesses with the few exceptions being when a lady's maid or seamstress was needed by a paying customer.

"I am here to meet my man of business. I do not see him, so he must have been delayed. We will require a quiet table away from any disturbances." George looked around for something quiet and very discreet.

"We have a private dining room available if you would prefer, sir." George would have corrected the young man identifying himself as a noble, but this was not the time or place. Anonymity was what was called for.

"That will be preferable. Lead the way." George waved him forward.

Twenty minutes later, Daniel Crossings was escorted to the private dining room.

"You are late, Crossings."

"My apologies, my lord. I was not at home when your message arrived. I only just received it and came right over." Daniel was not happy about being summoned so late in the evening. He had plans and this idiot was interfering with them.

He knew of the denial to transfer ownership of the Gables acreage and was expecting the summons, but not so quickly.

"You did not give my name, did you?" George's paranoia surfaced.

"I did not need to, my lord. I said I was meeting a business partner and they led me immediately to you." This was a conversation, for heaven's sake; they weren't committing a crime. What did this fool think would happen if they did know who he was?

"Very well. Sit down. First of all, what did you uncover regarding Mr. Smyth?"

"It appears Mr. Smyth and the Dowager Marchioness of Walsenburg were in Mariposa on the days in question.

"I spoke with several townsfolk who remember a man fitting Mr. Smyth's description in frantic search of a woman who had been abducted in Salassio. He spread quite a bit of gold and silver around searching for the missing lady.

"I could not locate anyone who knew where the woman was being held, but several witnesses did confirm a lady fitting the dowager marchioness's description took up residence at Willow House, on or about that time.

"There is only one parson in Mariposa, so finding the individual who officiated over the nuptials was not difficult.

"I spoke to the Reverend Samuel Thatcher. He, his wife, and his young daughter all confirmed the marriage of a Mr. Thomas Smyth to Analisa Elizabeth Childress-Hastings on twenty September in the year of our Lord, 1845." Daniel gave George a moment for all of this to sink in. "I saw the wedding registry. It is legitimated, my lord."

"That is preposterous! A woman matching my mother's description is not proof." He ran an unsteady hand through his hair. "Did you confirm her signature on the registry?"

"I could not, my lord. I am not familiar with your mother's signature." Daniel looked uncertain as to what to suggest next. "May I recommend a visit to Mariposa's parish by someone familiar with Her Ladyship's signature?"

George pondered his next step. This could not be true. He was expecting a quick unmasking of this sick joke and an expeditious dismissal of Mr. Thomas Smyth.

"The description they gave of the dowager marchioness was accurate. Even the fact that she appeared sickly and weak. And then there was the ring."

"What ring?" George did not recall a wedding ring. That was odd. His mother was not wearing a ring as was the custom.

"The wife and daughter both remember the lady's emerald ring. They described it as a large pear-shaped emerald with two concentric circles of diamonds set in fine gold."

Panic hit George like a bolt of lightning. The ring his father had given his mother when he proposed. As far back as he could remember, she had never had the ring off her finger. Although the description was vague, it was accurate enough to confirm it was his mother's ring they saw and his mother they met.

"I will consider sending someone to confirm her signature." What a disaster.

"Very good, my lord. How else can I be of service?" Daniel knew what was coming next.

"Are you aware of any complications in transferring ownership of the Gables acreage into Tenison's name?"

Of course he was. "I only know what Lord Abernathy's man of business shared with me." He had been practicing how he was going to address this question when it finally came.

"The assessor's office would only say the land was under scrutiny by the crown and its situation could not be altered under any circumstances until the inquiry was completed to the crown's satisfaction."

"That is mysterious and troubling. It is a mostly empty parcel of land. Why would the crown be concerned over who maintains ownership?" The comment was mostly introspective.

"Will there be anything else, my lord?" Daniel was anxious to leave before the marquess began asking questions. The less he talked, the less he would have to remember.

"Yes, yes. You are dismissed."

CHAPTER TWENTY-FIVE

Bellmorrow Estate, at the Sonastarian border

Analisa walked down to breakfast at just past eight in the morning. They'd been in Bellmorrow for three days and she'd begun to settle into a comfortable rhythm. She and Thomas always shared the morning and evening meals but were seldom together for the midday meal.

She walked into the morning room welcomed by the smell of fresh coffee and flaky pastries. The sun was just high enough to see, and only a few light and bright clouds floated past a tranquil backdrop just outside the large garden windows.

"Good morning, my lady." Powers was standing by her place at the other end of the table holding out her chair. "Did you sleep well, my lady?"

"I always sleep well in Bellmorrow, Powers. I am rejuvenated and ready for a glorious day." She looked around. "Where is Mr. Smyth this morning? Has he not yet risen?"

"I was informed by Mr. Smyth's valet he would be a few minutes late this morning. Would you care to wait before breaking your fast, my lady?"

"I would indeed. Would you please bring me some coffee and a copy of the *Observer?*"

She really wasn't interested in reading the local paper, but she wanted something to keep her busy while she waited for Thomas to join her.

She'd been reading some of the latest local gossip when Thomas entered the room. "Good morning, my dear. I must apologize. I was detained with a business matter." He took his place at the head of the table. "Have you eaten?"

"I have not." She signaled for Powers to begin serving. "Is this business anything over which I should be concerned?"

He seemed to have taken over her finances without a hesitation or a concern for her wishes. It was expected a husband would take full responsibilities for his wife's care and well-being but in most cases, it was his own money he was managing. In this case, the money belonged to her. No one seemed to give her a second thought. He had forced a fake marriage on her, taken charge of her properties and monies, making her a virtual dependent beggar of her own resources. Hopefully he'd be true to his word. When he had achieved his goal—whatever that was—he would grant her a divorce and her independence. Sure, he would steal from her but that was the price she had to pay to get out of this situation. She could afford it. What choice did she really have?

"Nothing to concern yourself over." Powers served him his usual eggs, ham, and fish. Like Analisa, he preferred coffee to tea, limiting himself to a small serving of something sweet at each meal.

"I would like to make a visit to Artemisia early this afternoon," She wasn't sure what his reaction would be to her independent request, but she had little to lose.

He knew she was anxious to pay a call on Miles Granger to discuss the Barony of Pennington situation in detail. To her credit, she refrained from mentioning the barony at any time except during their occasional private walks in the formal gardens.

"I think that is a wonderful idea." He knew he'd shocked her. "We can leave for Artemisia as soon as you can make yourself ready."

"I can be ready in three-quarters of an hour's time."

"Wonderful."

They finished their meal and Analisa hurried upstairs to change.

Within the hour he watched her descend the main staircase wearing a sapphire blue day dress with a matching bonnet. She was a vision, looking nowhere near her actual age. She would easily pass for thirty if she was a day.

"You look lovely, my dear." He held his arm out to her.

She gave him a look of skepticism. "Thank you, sir."

Laughing out loud, he challenged, "You do not believe me?" He patted her hand as it gently lay on his arm. "I believe you are one of the most beautiful women I have ever met. When have I ever hesitated to compliment you?"

"I appreciate the compliment, sir, but I am always wary of its purpose."

"Shall we?" He motioned toward the door.

"By all means."

It was just over an hour's ride to Fern Valley across the bridge in Artemisia. The coach seemed to know the way.

They arrived at a small but respectable two-story office building located on one of the city's main roads. Everyone around them was fashionably dressed and in a great hurry.

Thomas assisted Analisa from the coach, giving her a moment to get her bearings. She immediately saw several shops advertising some of the most beautiful dresses she'd ever seen. Many of the designs were more daring than she was willing to wear, but they were certainly beautiful.

She was aware Artemisia was more progressive than Sonastare in many ways. If true, her right to inherit the title of baroness based on bloodline rather than through marriage was a significant step forward as far as she was concerned.

"This way, my dear." Thomas guided her into the building's reception area.

A young man behind a small reception desk stood as they entered. "Good day, sir, madam. How may I assist you?"

"We are here to see Mr. Miles Granger. We are Mr. and Mrs. Thomas Smyth."

The young man referenced the open ledger on his desk. "Yes, sir. You are expected and welcome." He came from behind the desk to stand before them. "If you will follow me, I will escort you to Mr. Granger's offices."

Taking them up a short but wide flight of stairs, he was careful to keep a slower pace than he was accustomed to using. To the left and at the very end of the hall waited a tall, athletic-looking man in his mid-thirties. When they got closer, he stepped forward. "Good day to you, Mr. Smyth, my lady."

He addressed them as if unsure and looked to Thomas for confirmation.

"Good day to you, Mr. Granger. I do not believe you have had the pleasure of meeting my wife."

Miles turned to face Analisa, gave her a deep and elegant bow. "It is an honor to finally meet you, my lady."

"The pleasure is mine, Mr. Granger, but I am afraid the deference is misplaced. I am simply Mrs. Smyth now."

Miles smiled and allowed them to precede him into his office. "Adam," he addressed their young escort, "please have coffee brought up in fifteen minutes."

"It will be done, Mr. Granger." The young man departed, leaving them alone.

Miles closed the door behind him. "Please have a seat. Make yourselves comfortable."

He walked back behind his enormous mahogany partner's desk and took a seat.

"To what do I owe the pleasure of this visit?" He looked from one to the other.

Analisa looked to Thomas and he nodded his acquiescence.

"If I may be candid, Mr. Granger?" Miles nodded for her to continue. "I was unsure how to approach this delicate subject and how much knowledge I should divulge." She took a breath. "However, seeing that you were expecting us, I would like for you to tell me everything regarding the Barony of Pennington and how I am involved."

He looked to Thomas. "How much has already been shared with you, my lady?"

"Just the rudimentary facts, I assume. The title comes down from my mother's family, my mother being the thirteenth Baroness Pennington. Upon her death, I became the fourteenth baroness. Is this correct?"

"It is correct, my lady." He inclined forward in his chair. "The barony is an ancient one, dating back to the Gains Dynasty in 1066. Your ancestor, the first Baron Pennington, was cousin to Herron the Good. He was awarded the barony to secure a strategic stronghold in Artemisia in the event of an attack.

"The barony originally encompassed lands on both sides of the Mara River but has, over time, divested itself of significant holdings.

"When Her Grace, the late Duchess of Colton, inherited, the barony was not much more than a few thousand square miles of farmland, three wool mills, and a few mineral mines. It did and still owns the Mara River Port, but it collected low revenues due to long-term and well-established leases with local merchants. It would be fair to assume there are few in Artemisia who are aware the Pennington Barony exists.

"Your father, God rest his soul, saw the advantage of this anonymity and obscurity. He came to me with a plan to use the barony as an instrument for investment and prosperity. As your parents' representative here in Artemisia, I would look for lucrative opportunities in our kingdom and advise him on how and when to invest.

"Five years ago, in 1840, the twin kingdoms signed the Treaty of Faith, removing overall economic barriers, among others, those between Artemisia and Sonastare. Since then, I have been working with a colleague in Sonastare representing a very select group of investors. Your parents being my primary clients. We would identify profitable opportunities in both kingdoms, negotiate terms, and invest in our clients' names."

Analisa knew of the treaty, of course. But she was unaware of her parents' involvement in this level of investing. Was Darston involved? "Mr. Granger, not to digress; was the late Marquess of Walsenburg one of your clients?"

"Your late husband was, indeed, one of our clients. Your father brought him into the consortium. Access to our resources is by invitation only, you understand."

"I see. I assume all of his assets were included as part of my son's inheritance when he assumed the title upon his father's death?"

"Almost all. The Bellmorrow estate was purchased through a gentleman's agreement between your late father and your late husband but was bequeathed to you upon the marquess's death. Your father's family has owned the grand estate since 1736."

"I did not realize." This was a great deal to take in all at once.

"It was by design, I assure you." Miles reached for a map and opened it on his desk. "You see this area here?" He made a circle with his finger encompassing the lands on the east bank of the Mara River. "All of this land is currently Pennington. Now this tract, in addition to this parcel and this area here, all originally belonged to Pennington as well.

"In 1203, it was all the subject of a massive land grab, becoming part of the kingdom of Sonastare. Most of it was divided up and sold for profit to support the various conflicts we experienced over the years."

Analisa looked confused as she studied the map. She recognized the property he was identifying. "But is this all not part of the Bellmorrow estate as we know it today?"

Miles and Thomas both smiled. "It is, but it had to be reacquired in small pieces. Your father and mother knew you would inherit the Barony of Pennington some day and wanted to bring the barony back to what it once was. However, your father did not want to invest too heavily in Sonastare for fear of shedding too much light on your mother's and your connection to the barony. Moreover, he did not want anyone but you to inherit what he felt was your just birthright.

"He and your late husband came to the agreement, the marquess would purchase Bellmorrow from the duke. The estate was not entailed, so it was perfectly legal. Your husband would then slowly acquire what was originally part of the Barony of Pennington, gifting it to you upon his death. We gave the plan a code name."

"The Cloisters," Analisa voiced absently.

"That is correct, my lady."

"Mr. Granger?" She was now scrutinizing the map very closely. "Does this mean the Barony of Pennington is now back to its original glory and that I own it?"

A knock at the door made Miles rise. "If you will excuse me for a moment, my lady." He opened the door, allowing Adam in carrying a tray of coffee and biscuits. Once everyone had been served, Adam retired, leaving them alone once again.

Miles returned to the desk and picked up where they had left off. "All is Pennington but this acreage here, my lady." He pointed to a large tract of land just north of Bellmorrow running along the Mara River. "This parcel is currently under dispute. It has been used as open grazing land by villagers and residents for generations; it has long been assumed the Walsenburg Marquisate retains ownership, but a recent audit is raising doubts." He looked again at Thomas. "The Sonastarian crown was recently made aware of the situation and is investigating the matter."

"Is my son aware that there is an investigation underway?" George never mentioned it, but it may explain his sour mood of late.

"I cannot say, my lady. I am not as knowledgeable regarding Sonastarian politics as I am with the goings-on in Artemisia."

Analisa sat back, extremely overwhelmed. "Are those dependent on the barony well taken care of? Are there any glaring issues that need to be addressed with urgency?"

"Nothing demanding immediate attention, my lady. Rest assured you have an army of qualified and devoted retainers carefully selected to cover any need facing the barony. Your tenants are happy, loyal, and well cared for."

"Good. Now, what is our next step? I assume we need to file with the Artemisian crown recognizing me as the fourteenth Baroness Pennington?"

"That has all been taken care of, my lady. Although you have yet to be presented at court, you are and have officially been recognized as the fourteenth Baroness Pennington."

"So, I will now live a carefree life as Baroness Pennington? It cannot be as simple as that."

"Unfortunately, you are correct. The information is coming closer and closer to leaking out to the public with each passing day. I would encourage us to get ahead of this. If we control the dissemination, we will have greater leverage in controlling the fallout."

"What would you suggest, Mr. Granger?"

"I would suggest you both go home and discuss the situation. I have given you much to think about in a very short time. You must take some time to come to terms with all we have shared. We can meet again in a few days and consider strategies. Does that sound reasonable to you, my lady?"

"It does indeed, Mr. Granger. Thank you for your considerations in this matter as well as for your loyalty to my family for so many years."

"It has been and continues to be my honor, my lady." Miles stood, followed closely by Thomas and Analisa. "I will show you out."

The coach ride back to Bellmorrow was sobering. Thomas had suggested they stay a little longer in Fern Valley. They could do some shopping and enjoy a midday meal. Analisa just wanted to get back to the manor and rest. She thought he'd insist to delay their departure but was pleasantly surprised when he agreed to return immediately.

"Did you know about all of this?" He had told her much of this tale prior to their return to Salassio, but there was obviously much more to tell.

He looked out the window for a moment. "I am very good at what I do. Yes, I knew all of this months ago." Turning back to face her, he grinned, appearing to be enjoying the distress this was causing her. "There is much more to tell. You have only been exposed to the overture. The play is about to unfold with the opening act being the announcement and your first formal and official appearance as Baroness Pennington."

"I suppose you have this all planned and orchestrated?"

"I do indeed. I am very much looking forward to being recognized as Baron, Lord Pennington. It has a nice ring to it, I believe. What do you think?"

Disgusting was what she thought of it all. "How is the opening act, as you put it, supposed to take place?"

"It is already in the works, my dear. Notifications are being drafted and will be forwarded to both the Sonastarian and the Artemisian parliaments. The Marquess of Walsenburg and the Duke of Colton will also be officially informed. You should be receiving your formal announcement by special messenger within two days.

"We will throw a grand ball at Bellmorrow a week from Friday next, when we will be formally introduced to Sonastarian society as the reining Baron and Baroness Pennington. A similar celebration will take place at Dunnfee Court on the Pennington estate in Artemisia the following Friday.

"We will, of course, need a whole new wardrobe befitting our rank and status. A couturier will be at Bellmorrow in the morning to take your measurements. New coaches have been ordered bearing the Pennington crest.

"We will relocate to Dunnfee Court, where we will take up residence as noble citizens of Artemisia. The estate will need upgrades and renovations. But most importantly, you will need to be presented at the Artemisian court. This will solidify our position, opening many political doors in both kingdoms. A dream come true, would you not agree? You are once again Lady Analisa with a devoted and loving husband at your side. It is every young girl's fantasy."

"Do not dare pretend to take any credit for this, my Lord Claudius." She was livid. "All of this would still have taken place with or without your extortion and coercion."

"Not the devoted and loving husband part of it, my lady." He leaned forward and lowered his voice to just above a whisper. "Do not let any of this go to your head, my dear. The rules we established at the beginning of this little adventure are still very much in place. This can go from a fairy tale to a nightmare in a snap. Be a good girl. Behave yourself and all will be well."

She didn't doubt he meant what he said. He himself could go from hero to villain in the blink of an eye, why not the situation?

The remainder of the journey passed in complete silence.

CHAPTER TWENTY-SIX

Bellstrand Island, Sonastare

"Joseline!" George bellowed as he entered the dining room. "You will not believe this recent bit of news. My mother is the heir to the Pennington Barony of Artemisia. She will be presented to the Artemisian court as the fourteenth Baroness Pennington within a fortnight." He extended the missive to her.

"Baroness?" Joseline was almost speechless. "Who? How? Your family has no ties to Artemisia."

"Apparently we do. According to this report, my grandmother, the late Duchess of Colton, had deep roots in Artemisia. She inherited the title over ten years ago. With Mother as her sole heir, Mother assumed the title upon her death."

"That is not possible, George." Joseline was beside herself. "She is a woman. Women are prevented from assuming noble titles other than through marriage."

"Ah, but the rules are different in Artemisia. Women can inherit." He took back the letter and read it again.

Just then, Dobbs entered the dining room. "My lord, the Duchess of Welby, Viscountess Cross, and Baroness Kelt are here to see you. I have shown them to the family library."

George looked to Joseline. "They must have heard the news as well. Let us greet them." He turned and walked toward the family library, not waiting for his wife to join him.

Their three guests were standing and frantically speaking all at once when George entered the library with Joseline following closely behind.

"Ladies! To what do we owe this visit?"

"As if you do not know." Ada dared him to deny it.

"Ah! You must have received news of Mother's rise to the Pennington Barony."

"I would not exactly call it a 'rise,' George. She is the daughter of a duke and the wife of a marquess. It is more of an assumption than an ascension." Marie thought it quite a clever play on words.

Joseline was not amused. "She has just gone from being a Mrs. Nobody to a baroness. I would certainly consider that a rise."

All four, including George, were shocked at the statement. Everyone had the good manners not to comment. The atmosphere turned from jovial to sobering in the blink of an eye.

"Yes, you do have a point, my lady." Maggie gave Joseline her most refined, manicured smile. "Please excuse our unannounced visit. We can blame it on the excitement of the moment."

George and Joseline could actually feel the temperature in the room dropping by the second. "Not at all, my lady." He attempted to take the chill off. "Please join us in breaking your fast if you have not already done so. Maybe some tea or coffee if you would prefer."

"That is very kind of you, my lord." Marie stepped forward. "We have already eaten, and we won't take up much more of your valuable time. We have all received word from the new baroness that there is to be a ball Friday at Bellmorrow to present the new Baron and Baroness Pennington to society. We are planning on traveling together, depart-ing at first light, reaching Bellmorrow on Thursday afternoon the day before the ball. We were wondering if you would care to join the caravan?"

A ball? This was the first he'd heard of it. He'd be obligated to attend. "That sounds wonderful, ladies. I could not ask for a better escort than to have my mother's closest and dearest friends to accompany us."

"I am not certain I could be ready in time. It is very short notice." Joseline did not want to go but knew she had an obligation to attend. She had already made a huge blunder with her recent comment. Crying off would not do her status or reputation any good. These ladies had significant influence with Sonastarian society. "Perhaps I can make it work." She gave George her most sympathetic look. "After all, we really should be by your mother's side to support her through this auspicious event." These old biddies were an irritation, but their support was essential.

The Duchess of Welby stepped forward and took Joseline's hand in hers with a pat. "I will not hear of it. You are increasing and much too delicate for such an arduous journey. We all feel you should remain here where you can receive plenty of rest. We would never forgive ourselves if anything should happen to endanger the health or welfare of the next heir of Walsenburg."

If there was any affection or genuine concern in the duchess's speech, Joseline and George both missed it. Joseline bit her upper lip in a nervous reaction. She could almost taste the venom.

Ada stepped back, joining Marie and Maggie just behind her. "Well, we will be on our way. Please send word if you will be joining us, my lord. We leave promptly at sunup." All three ladies began walking toward the door.

With a sudden stop, Ada looked over her shoulder toward where the Marquess and Marchioness of Walsenburg stood dumbfounded with mouths slightly agape. Without turning fully around to face them, "Do we no longer show a duchess proper courtesies and respect on Bellstrand?"

Still aghast, George bowed and Joseline dipped into a formal curtsy. Ada looked at Maggie. "What has become of the younger generation?"

Marie nodded her head. "Perhaps we should publish a small pocket reference they can carry with them on how to properly conduct themselves in public."

"That will not do much good with some, my dear." Maggie gave Joseline an all-encompassing and appraising look. Scrunched her face as if smelling something offensive, she concluded, "When you consider the background and lineage of some of our new nobles, their shortcomings are to be expected. However, I am simply not sure if they are to be tolerated."

They continued to the front door and out to their awaiting coaches.

George had never been to the Arctic, but it had been described to him in bone-chilling detail. The temperature could not possibly be any cooler there than in his library at this very moment.

In one off-the-cuff, catty discussion, these three had not only put Joseline on notice but her entire family as well. Just another nail in his social coffin as things were developing. He had to find a way of turning things around.

The constraints surrounding the transfer of title to the Gables acreage had not been resolved. He had made inquiries, cashing in on what few favors he had owed him, but he had gotten no further in settling the matter. All he knew was that the acreage was under investigation by the crown.

Getting out of town for a few days was not a bad idea. Tenison would have to wait.

CHAPTER TWENTY-SEVEN

Bellmorrow Estate, at the Sonastarian Border

It was the day before the ball. Bellmorrow Manor was in a frenzy of activity. Every floor, wall, and banister had been cleaned to within an inch of its life. Wood polished, glass sparkling, curtains and carpets aired. The flower arrangements were being placed and the kitchen had additional staffing working around the clock.

Most of the guests had been arriving over the past few days, but Analisa's most important guests—her family and friends—were still en route. Her cousin, the Duke of Colton, had arrived the previous day, but she had not seen him for more than a few minutes when he arrived and at dinner last evening. They did not have much time to converse, but they really weren't close.

Sonastare's prime minister was due this morning and all anxiously awaited his arrival. He would be representing the kingdom and the royal family.

It was just past six in the morning when Tully knocked on her sitting room door. "Pardon me, my lady, I was sent to let you know Prime Minister Arcady has arrived and awaits you in the main library."

Analisa was just completing a letter. "Please inform Baron Pennington I will join him, and we can go down together."

"Immediately, my lady." Tully bobbed a curtsy and left.

"You certainly look every bit a baroness, my lady." Thomas was waiting for her at the top of the staircase as she came down the hall. "Is that one of the new gowns?"

She looked down and ran a hand over the skirt. "Not new exactly but certainly upgraded. Only a few gowns could be completed prior to tomorrow's event. I requested a few I had be modified to fit the moment."

"For what we are paying, they should hire an army of seamstresses and tailors to have our wardrobes completed by day's end."

"For what 'we' are paying?" She gave him a skeptical stare.

He offered her his arm and together they descended the stairs.

Entering the main library, they found Prime Minister Arcady perusing a book he'd pulled off the shelf. He closed the book and bowed with a smile. "*Hamlet*." He held up the tome. "It has been a while since I have had time to enjoy a good book. Mr. Shakespeare is a favorite of mine."

Analisa took a closer look at the title. "Welcome to our home, Your Grace." She curtsied and Thomas bowed. "It is an honor to have you with us."

"The honor is mine, my lady. On behalf of His Majesty, may I congratulate you and the baron. We are looking forward to you joining us at the Fortalesa Palace, where he may convey his felicitations personally."

"Will you sit down, Your Grace? May we offer you some tea or coffee? Maybe something cool to drink." Thomas led him to the leather wingback chair by the settee.

He gave Thomas a steady stare. "Something cool would be most welcomed. Thank you," he hesitated for an instant, "my lord."

Thomas motioned for a maid to approach. "Carol, would you bring His Grace a cold glass of lemonade please?" The maid bobbed a curtsy and left.

Had the prime minister taken a dislike to Thomas? Analisa wondered. One did not achieve the position of prime minister without intuitions. Did this astute man perceive the deception? Could he see the devil behind the angel's mask?

If she could find an opportunity to speak with the prime minister privately and candidly explain her plight, he may be the only one available who could help her end this odyssey.

She and Thomas sat together on the settee. "I, too, am a devoted follower of Mr. Shakespeare, Your Grace." She looked at Thomas for a moment. He did not appear to notice the prime minister's skepticism. "I see you have chosen *Hamlet*. Is it your favorite of his works?"

"My favorite is *King Lear*, my lady, but *Hamlet* does come in a close second." He handed the book to Analisa. "I vicariously enjoy the intrigue of its characters. At the same time, I am grateful I do not have to deal with that level of deception and treachery in my day-to-day life."

"You are fortunate indeed, Your Grace." She could not resist the temptation. "What do you think of Shakespeare's character Claudius?"

"While I cannot condone his actions, I must admit; I admire his resolve."

"Well, we will not keep you, Your Grace. I know you must be exhausted after your journey and in need of rest." Thomas waved over a footman who had been waiting patiently by the door. "Foster will show you to your rooms, Your Grace. You are welcome to join us for the midday meal or we can have a tray sent up. Dinner is at six thirty in the main dining room." He turned to the footman. "Foster, if you would."

The footman bowed and motioned the prime minister to precede him from the library.

Thomas approached Analisa carefully. "Interviewing allies, my dear?"

She stood and faced him. "One never knows when an ally will come in handy." She picked up her skirt and walked past him. "If you will excuse me, my Lord Claudius, there is still much to be done before the ball."

"Is there anything I can do?"

"You have done enough, my lord." She was gone.

CHAPTER TWENTY-EIGHT

The manor had just come into view. "How lovely!" Marie was as excited as a young girl at Christmastime. "I had forgotten the splendor of Bellmorrow."

"I was under the impression you had visited here before, my dear." Marie's husband Lord Ernesto Grossman, Baron Kelt, was a gentle man who doted on his beloved wife. When she said "we are off to Bellmorrow," he simply followed.

He wasn't weak by any definition of the word. In fact, in political circles, Lord Kelt was a rather frightening figure. In one word, powerful. But he had one Achilles' heel—his wife.

They had met when her coach broke its rear axle. He was riding by, and was left motionless as he watched a beautiful young woman, in a seafoam green silk gown, ankle deep in mud, help three liveried men attempt to repair the damage. He had no idea how long he'd been standing there when he heard her speak. To him? "This is not a theater and we are not performers, sir. If you are not going to help, please move along, else I will insist you pay admission for the performance."

That was it. He dismounted and helped get the coach back on its way. They were married the following year and started an endless honeymoon that had so far lasted twenty-three years.

"I was here only once on holiday more years past than I will admit to." She gave him the coquettish look that never failed to brighten his world.

"It could not possibly be more than twenty years past. I can certainly understand why you would not remember. Infants do not enjoy long-term memories."

"I would advise you not to flirt with me too outrageously, kind sir. My husband is a very jealous man."

"He must be a bit addlepated allowing you out of his sight for even a moment."

"How dare you speak of my husband in that manner. I will have you know he is the smartest, kindest, strongest, and most handsome man on God's green earth." She hit him with her closed fan. "You will apologize immediately or face the consequences."

"And if I refuse to apologize?"

"I will have no choice but to deal with you most severely." The coach door opened. "Live in fear until I deal out your punishment."

He was smiling very broadly as a footman assisted Marie out of the coach.

They joined the Duke and Duchess of Welby and Viscount and Viscountess Cross under the portico as an army of footmen began unloading their coaches.

"Shall we?" The duke gestured toward the front doors.

Powers was happily awaiting them in the foyer as they entered.

"Your Graces, my lords and ladies." He bowed as low as he could manage in his advanced years. "It is a pleasure to see you. I hope you all had a pleasant journey."

Ada was the first to speak. "We are so happy to be here, Powers. I understand the baroness must be quite busy, but is there any chance we may see her even for a moment before we lock ourselves away as is proper?"

Powers leaned in conspiratorially. "The baroness left strict instruction she was to be notified the instant you arrived. She has scheduled a private celebration in the family wing for just the immediate family. If you are not too exhausted from traveling, Your Grace."

The three women were almost giddy with joy. "Lead the way, kind sir," Maggie encouraged.

The east end of the second level of the manor had been designated the family wing. Two massive ornate oak doors separated this section from the rest of the floor and the house.

Once in the family wing, turn right and you'd run into the master's chambers at the end of the hall. Turn left, and you'd walk directly into the most elegant family room you could imagine.

As they entered, they were greeted by half a dozen maids and footmen carrying trays of confections and refreshments. Coffee and tea were just being brought in.

"Please make yourselves comfortable. If there is anything more you require, please let one of the footmen know and it will be taken care of immediately. Her Ladyship will be with you shortly." He had no time to bow when Analisa appeared behind him.

"Her Ladyship is here." Analisa was enveloped by six sisterly arms in a most unfashionable manner. "Good Lord! It has been an age since we last saw each other."

"It seems whenever we part, something monumental happens to you, Ana." Ada stepped back. "First you are abducted, return married, and now you are dubbed Baroness Pennington."

"Trust me. It is all out of my control." The four of them walked as one unit to the sitting area with their loving husbands all trailing obediently. They were comfortable with the formula. When these four women united, everyone and everything melted away.

Analisa suddenly realized they weren't the only four in the room.

"Gentlemen. How rude of me. Thank you for coming to my grand debut. And for bringing my dearest friends with you. It would be a sad affair without them."

134

Before anyone could respond, Thomas entered, looking every bit the baron. "How wonderful. Everyone has arrived safe and sound." He walked over to greet his guests. "Your Grace, my lords." He turned toward the all-female cast. "My ladies." He gave them all a formal bow.

They dispensed with the pleasantries in short order. Thomas offered, "Gentlemen, let us adjourn to the billiard room for cigars and brandy. I realize it's a bit early in the day, but we are here to rejoice, and it is never too early or too late to celebrate, would you not say?"

The men departed, the staff disappeared, and the doors closed. Now they could talk.

Ada took one hand and Maggie the other while Marie pulled one of the chairs closer. "Out with it. I want to hear every little detail of this sordid story from beginning to end." Ada looked very concerned.

"There is really nothing sordid about it. But it is rather complicated." She thought for a moment. Where to begin?

Thomas had brought the men to an immense billiard room. It was called the billiard room due to the two billiard tables dominating the space. The room, however, was more of an entertainment room. It could effortlessly be converted to a card room, a space fit for parlor games, and with some creativity, a small theater where children could and had over the years performed to the delight of their family and friends.

They were into their second game of billiards when the prime minister entered. "My apologies for disturbing you in your private quarters, my lord, but I would like a moment of your time if possible."

Thomas stepped forward to conduct the introductions. "Your Grace, my lords; you all know Prime Minister Aguste Arcady?" All gave a nod.

"A pleasure to see you here, Your Grace. I do not remember when last we met for purposes other than to argue politics. It is wonderful to be with you in a more relaxed setting." Ernesto gave a bow and extended his hand in greeting.

"We do not seem to celebrate enough these days, Lord Kelt."

"If you will join me in my study, Your Grace." Thomas waved him toward the doors.

"Gentlemen." The prime minister gave them each a nod and led the way toward Thomas's study.

Analisa had told her entire story. She had even shared with them the sordid details of her supposed marriage to Mr. Thomas Smyth, now Baron Pennington.

"So, are you actually married or is this all an elaborate ruse to separate you from your money?" Ada was the problem solver of the group.

"If we married it was by proxy. However, he has placed me in a very difficult situation. I can fight him and possibly win but at a very high cost. We have been living as man and wife for several weeks." Ana looked defeated.

"There are only two options open to us in ending this union with your reputation intact: the marriage is dissolved through divorce or annulment, or you become a widow for a second time in as many years." Marie was the impulsive one of the group. She led with her heart not her brain. "I like option two the best."

"That is all well and good, dearest, but 'light skirt' is a more acceptable moniker than 'murderess.'" Maggie was the logical thinker. She would ponder the details of a problem, visiting every possible consequence before she would settle on a plan of action.

"Has he offered you any options?"

"He has. If I 'behave myself,' as he puts it, he promises to divorce me for a settlement and allow me to continue my life with little trace of him and no interference."

"And how long is this faux marriage intended to last?" Ada needed a target date.

"That he will not commit to. I believe there are events taking place behind the scenes he will not share with me." Analisa felt much better simply having shared the situation with them. She knew she could trust them implicitly. Their husbands as well. They would not do anything that might jeopardize the situation.

"Does he intend on taking all of your money? That, we can take steps to prevent without his knowledge."

"Honestly, I am not so much worried over the money as I am over potential harm to you or to my children. I do not know how much he has already syphoned from my coffers or how much more he intends on taking. But I would gladly give it all up if we all emerge from this unscathed."

"I will speak to William this evening. He will know how best to proceed inconspicuously." Ada's husband, William Robelight, Duke of Welby, had strong connections at court. As did Marie's and Maggie's husbands. "Who did they send to represent the crown?"

"His Grace the prime minister arrived yesterday."

"Good. There are few men sharper than Aguste Arcady." Ada was well acquainted with Sonastare's prime minister. He was honest and very well respected in both kingdoms.

Analisa absently began to wring her hands. "I intended on gaining a private audience with His Grace while he was here."

"No need for you to take that kind of risk. William and I will speak with him on your behalf." Ada reached out stopping Ana's nervous motions.

Analisa looked around at each familiar and beloved face. "I do not know how I would get through this without you all." They all came in to one huge hug. "I love you all so very much."

CHAPTER TWENTY-NINE

The ball was well underway. George and Joseline had arrived late the previous night and had slept in most of the day.

Tap, tap, tap. Thomas focused everyone's attention on the dais, where he and Analisa stood. "We would like to welcome you all to our home. Many of you have traveled a great distance with very little notice to join us in celebration. To our dear friends and family, your presence here this evening means the world to us." He looked around, finding a sea of elated faces staring back at him. All but three, who stood very close together shooting daggers in his direction.

"I would like to now introduce our prime minister, who will do us the honor of the presentation." He gestured to his right. "My lords and ladies, it is my honor to present His Grace, Aguste Arcady, Prime Minister of Sonastare."

With all the dignity of a royal, Aguste stepped on to the dais. "Good evening, my lords and ladies. On behalf of Their Highnesses King Maximilien, Queen Shahjalal, and the entire royal family, I am honored to welcome Baron and Baroness Pennington of Artemisia to our kingdom." Everyone clapped. "May their reign continue to bring unity and peace to the twin kingdoms for many years to come." The applause continued. Many rushed to the dais to congratulate and welcome Thomas and Analisa into the Elite. For most it was merely ceremonial. Analisa had been an Elite since birth. Thomas, even with the title, was still considered an outsider.

"Are you not going to join in the celebration?" Aguste asked, walking up to George and Joseline standing in the wings.

"Good evening, Your Grace." George gave a tight bow, Joseline a slight curtsy. "We thought it more appropriate to convey our felicitations privately. There are so many bidding for their attention, we do not wish to encroach on their time."

"That is very considerate of you."

"Your Grace, I recently sold some property not far from here to Viscount Abernathy. Unfortunately, the transfer of ownership was denied by the courts." George hesitated for a moment, attempting to appear nonchalant regarding the entire situation. "Would you have any idea why such a simple transaction would be held up?"

"I am afraid without more information I would not venture to guess." He took out his pocket watch. "If you will excuse me, my lord, my lady." With a nod and a smile, he was gone.

Damn it! What was going on?

Joseline stepped closer. "You sold property?"

"Useless grazing land just north of Bellmorrow. Nothing of any consequence."

The ball was a great success. Two orchestras played in concert while guests danced to a cool and welcomed breeze flowing through the airy ballroom. The crowd had died down some when Ada approached Analisa giving some last-minute instructions to Powers.

"We spoke with Arcady," she whispered in Analisa's ear.

The two of them caught Maggie's and Marie's eye. Analisa

motioned to the hall. They all met in the hall and followed Ana to the family wing and the private library.

Once inside with the doors closed, Ana relaxed her public façade. "What did he tell you?"

"He acknowledged our concerns and has promised to look into the matter."

Marie chimed in. "I spoke with Levander Finch, Count Chieveley just moments ago. He is a confidant of your son." Analisa was frantic for any information that may help her out of this situation. "He tells me George had Thomas's account of your rescue and subsequent marriage investigated."

"I knew George would get to the bottom of things. What did he uncover?"

"Well, I hate to dash your hopes, my dear, but it appears Thomas has done an exceptional job of covering his tracks." They all found places to sit. "George was counting on two key things. First, that the description of the lady in question did not match yours. Or that the signature on the marriage license was not written by your hand."

"Of course it was not me or my signature. I was not there."

"Well, although he could not confirm the signature, the description of the lady by several witnesses does seem to fit you perfectly." Marie looked as disappointed as Ana felt. "There is one other element of note. The parson's wife and daughter vividly remember your emerald ring." This hit Analisa like a thunderbolt. "They apparently described it in detail. And since the ring has never left your finger since Darston placed it there, George is convinced you were the woman at Mariposa and Thomas's legal wife."

Analisa took on a faraway look. *That is why he asked for my ring. Positive proof.*

"Listen to me. When we arrived at the cottage where I was to be held, my abductor took my emerald ring. Thomas returned it to me the morning we arrived back in Salassio."

Ana stood and began to pace. "He must have given it to a lookalike to wear. He is a clever man. Has anyone been dispatched to validate the signature on the marriage license?"

"There are only a few who would recognize your signature, Ana. It would have to be one of us, George, or Evelyn. Anyone else and we risk the secret being exposed." Maggie's mind was on the problem.

"William and I will go," Ada volunteered. "We will make some excuse about visiting Felicity's Gates in Eclipse. We can travel to and from Mariposa in under two days. Confirming the signature a fake, we can confront Thomas Smyth at Dunnfee Court before the celebration in Artemisia commences."

"Oh Ada! Would you do that for me?" Ana was in tears at this point as were they all.

"That and so much more, dearest." Many hugs and many more tears followed.

CHAPTER THIRTY

Most of the guests simply migrated from Bellmorrow to Dunnfee Court for the following week's ball held in Artemisia. It seemed a bit redundant to everyone, but it was ceremony. The crown had welcomed and recognized Analisa in Sonastare. The same was expected in Artemisia.

A few faces did change. Although the battles between the twin kingdoms were long since over, there was some residual resentment left with some of the more ancient names.

As much as they loved and respected Analisa, they would not bring themselves to set foot on Artemisian soil.

The same sentiment was prevalent in Artemisia. Many of the guests planning to partake in the celebration in Artemisia politely refused to attend the first ball held at Bellmorrow Manor in Sonastare.

The mood had been kept jovial, and the guests made a party of it all. On the journey from Bellmorrow to Dunnfee Court, several sight-seeing trips were scheduled.

The ancient Gains fortress, where Edward Malankaree, Viscount Lakeville defeated the western invaders.

The Abbey of St. Christopher and the majestic waterfalls at Dove Cliff.

The ninety-minute journey turned into an all-day event. No one could recall a time when traveling between the twin kingdoms was as enjoyable or as educational.

Arriving at Dunnfee Court, all made for their rooms. Servants had gone on ahead to prepare for their employers' arrival. Guests arrived to find their belongings stored away, their maids and retainers well familiar with the manor and its operations, a hot bath and a hot meal ready and waiting for them to enjoy.

Thomas and Analisa had arrived early that morning to make sure all was in readiness. Marie, Maggie, and their husbands all chose to cry off from the sightseeing events where George and Joseline partook of the festivities more to avoid interaction with Ana and any of her three close friends.

During George and Joseline's stay at Bellmorrow, they had not been given the cut direct. However, the ladies had made it crystal clear their insult of Ana had hurt deeply and had taken root. Their injustice would not be ignored or go unavenged.

William and Ada were due at Dunnfee Court the following morning and everyone was anxious for their findings.

"Who will be representing the Artemisian crown at the ball?" Maggie entered Ana's morning room with Marie in tow.

"Prime Minister Jerimiah Fellows."

"How exciting!" Marie helped herself to tea and some biscuits.

Everyone was doing their best to keep their minds and Ana's off Ada's pending return.

"Is there anything we can do to help you, Ana?" Maggie sat next to her. Analisa was completely distracted. "Ana?"

Her reverie broken, she gave herself a mental shake. "I am sorry, dear. I was woolgathering."

"You were obsessing over what Ada may or may not find at Mariposa's parish." Marie patted her hand. "You need to relax, or you will awaken to enormous bags under those beautiful eyes."

"It cannot be helped, I am afraid. This whole charade hangs on the fact that the signature on the marriage license is a fake."

Thomas took this very opportunity to enter the morning room. "Good morning, ladies. We are arranging a hunt for this afternoon. Would any of you care to join in the fun?"

"No thank you, Thomas. We need to go over some of the final details for the ball on Friday." He didn't look impressed. "Moreover, Prime Minister Fellows will be arriving in the early afternoon tomorrow, and I want everything to be to perfection for his first visit to Dunnfee Court."

"I quite understand, my dear. You will tell me if there is anything I can do to help you?" Ana smiled and nodded. He tipped his head to his audience. "Ladies. I hope you will have a pleasant day." He was gone.

Powers gave a light knock on Analisa's open door. Everyone put on their game faces. "Yes, Powers, what is it?"

"My apologies, my lady. There is a Mr. Granger downstairs who wishes an audience if you have a few moments."

"Yes of course. Please show him into the reception room. I will be down momentarily."

"Very good, my lady." They watched him leave. It wasn't that Powers could not be trusted. Analisa considered him family. It was simply a precaution. The fewer who knew, the safer they would be.

"Granger? That is the man of business for the barony, correct?"

"That he is. And a very intelligent man to boot." She stood, making her way to the door. "I will not be long, dears. Please stay and enjoy the peace and quiet while it lasts."

Analisa headed toward the reception room and the awaiting Mr. Granger.

"Good morning, my lady. I regret disturbing you. I was hoping to speak with the baron about these matters, but I was told he was not in."

Miles was more attractive than she remembered. "Good morning, Mr. Granger. No, my husband has gone hunting with several of our guests. To what do we owe the pleasure of your visit?"

He presented her with a stack of documents. "These will need to be signed by you and the baron prior to the prime minister's visit to-morrow afternoon. He will add his signature and send them ahead via courier to the parliament building for processing."

"And what exactly am I signing?"

"You will need to declare an heir and successor in the event of your death. If a successor is unknown, you may enter 'undeclared' in place of a name." He looked apologetic. "I regret I must bring this sobering subject up at this festive time, but it is a required formality."

"Out of curiosity, Mr. Granger, what would happen if I died listing my successor as 'undeclared'?"

"The baron would maintain his title and oversight over the Pennington Barony until a lawful successor could be located. If no suc-cessor was identified, the title would revert back to the crown upon his death."

"I see." Was Thomas planning on encouraging her to keep her suc-cessor undeclared? "Is my husband aware of this requirement?"

"He is, my lady."

"And has he made any recommendations as to who I should name as my successor?"

"He has not, my lady. Although he did comment your children are well provided for and in no need of what the barony has to offer."

"Thank you, Mr. Granger. We will have the documents ready for His Grace by the time he arrives."

Miles bowed. "Your servant, my lady." And took his leave.

CHAPTER THIRTY-ONE

The ball at Dunnfee Court had been almost a mirror image of the Bellmorrow ball. The vast majority of the guests had participated in both events, enjoying a departure from the day-to-day. Many commented it was more of an elaborate house party than two official balls. The entertainment and festivities lasted for almost a fortnight.

In the end, Analisa's concerns over naming her successor were for naught. She named her son, George Hastings, Marquess of Walsenburg as her obvious heir. There were no objections from Thomas.

It was Wednesday following the Dunnfee Court ball, and everything seemed to be quickly returning to normal.

The additional staff hired for the merriments was dismissed after being handsomely compensated and complimented.

Analisa and Thomas had remained at Dunnfee Court, along with Powers, Tully, and several of Analisa's loyal retainers.

Thomas had given Bruce a permanent position as valet, and a few additional positions were created and staffed.

Their complete wardrobe had arrived along with three new coaches, all emblazoned with the Pennington crest.

Thomas had discussed restocking the stables as well as their adjacent forest reserves and ponds.

PANEQUE Y DIAZ

Contractors had been providing much-needed repairs and up-grades to the manor as well as to several of the tenant homes and farms.

Agricultural upgrades were discussed while modernization for both Dunnfee Court and Bellmorrow were now in the planning stages.

William and Ada had returned from Mariposa with less than encouraging news. They had carefully scrutinized the signature on the wedding registry. The signatures were not identical, but they were close enough that proving fraud would be difficult.

Analisa was becoming more and more agitated as she felt the marital trap closing in on her. Part of her agitation was her constantly changing opinion of Thomas.

He had kept his word, never forcing himself on her, although she suspected frequent illicit encounters with any number of female members on her staff. He was an exceptionally beautiful man. He would be a temptation to any female with a pulse. No, that was not a concern as long as he kept his liaisons discreet.

On the contrary, her vexation was his proactive approach to the title. He had been fully involved in restoring the barony to its original glory. He seemed, dare she acknowledge it, downright selfless. Yet he never missed an opportunity to keep her in her place as the subservient wife. She was not allowed to question his decisions in public and he never requested her permission or feedback before acting on his impulses.

As much as she condemned his motives, she admired and appreciated his actions, being impressed with their results.

I must speak with Mr. Granger. Thomas was to parts unknown. This was the perfect opportunity.

She called for her coach and changed into one of her more beautiful new day dresses for the visit.

Within the hour she was on her way to Fern Valley to pay an unannounced call on Mr. Miles Granger.

148

"The Baroness Pennington to see you, sir." Adam Stewart, Miles's young assistant, stepped aside, allowing Analisa to enter.

"I apologize for arriving without a prior appointment, Mr. Granger. I offered to wait but your assistant insisted you would see me right away. I hope this is not a huge inconvenience." Analisa was polite but determined.

"There is no inconvenience, my lady. Please have a seat." He waited until she had made herself comfortable before taking his seat behind the desk. "Can I offer you anything, my lady?"

"That is very kind of you but that will not be necessary."

"What can I do for you today, my lady?"

"You will forgive my bluntness, Mr. Granger, but I do not have a great deal of time and I need answers." She looked at him as if assessing his trustworthiness. "May I confide in you, sir?"

"It would depend on the confidence, my lady. I cannot be a party to anything unlawful or unjust."

Analisa laughed. "Fair enough." She relaxed, satisfied she could place her trust in this man. Her father and her husband had trusted him and as far as she was aware, he had not betrayed that trust.

"I need to know what amount has been spent on behalf of the barony. Is this a subject over which you have some knowledge?"

"As it stands, my lady, until you choose a new man of business or choose to manage the affairs of the barony yourselves, I am probably the only person on earth with a comprehensive knowledge of the financial comings and goings of the barony."

"Excellent. I would like an accounting of all monies in and out of the barony's portfolio."

"How far back do you wish to go, my lady?"

"For the moment, just the past month. At some point in the future,

I would like to see the ledgers for all transactions conducted in the past two years since my parents' death."

"The past month we can go over today if your schedule permits. It will take me some time to gather the necessary ledgers and documents covering the past two years."

"I am at your disposal, sir. Lead on."

They spent most of the morning and part of the afternoon poring over each and every transaction. Aside from the wardrobe Thomas had purchased for himself and a very expensive thoroughbred stallion, there were pieces of jewelry she had not seen, and several transactions labeled "personal entertainment" she could not begin to guess at. Well, she could guess but preferred not to.

There were six mysterious entries labeled "personal investments" that alarmed her. They were irregular entries with the smallest amount being for twelve thousand in local currencies.

Good Lord! At this rate he would have the barony bankrupt inside of a year.

"Mr. Granger, what are these six transactions covering?"

"I am not privy to that information, my lady. They were made by the baron personally. It is not my place to question him or to demand justifications."

"You may not demand justifications, but I certainly will." She stood ramrod straight. "Is there anything I can do to curtail or hinder any future such expenses?"

"Unfortunately, there is nothing you can do legally, my lady. He is the Baron Pennington and, as such, maintains unfettered access and authority over the barony's assets."

"But the title is mine not his. He enjoys a marital privilege and a courtesy title at best."

"As the law exists today, you can file with the courts to deny him authority over barony assets. As you correctly stated, you are the rightful heir.

"This condition is much easier if filed as part of the marital contract and agreed to by both parties. A post-marital codicil of this type is more difficult unless the baron agrees to give up his authorities. You will need to prove grounds."

"Grounds? Is not being a wastrel, a spendthrift, a squanderer, and a thief grounds enough?"

"It may be if it can be incontrovertibly proven, my lady. Unfortunately, that will take a great deal of time and evidence."

"What are my more realistic options?"

"I only know of two that will grant you immediate success; they would be mental incompetence and treason. Unfortunately, you will still face the same burden. Incontrovertible proof."

"I find this unacceptable, Mr. Granger. There must be something we can do to keep this man from destroying the barony. From obliterating all my father and husband worked so hard to achieve."

"I regret I do not have any options to offer you, my lady."

Analisa had this feeling of falling. As if she had been pushed off a very tall mountain and was heading to the bottom of a very dark pit. As it appeared, a bottomless pit.

CHAPTER THIRTY-TWO

Bellstrand Island, Sonastare

It was mid-October when Count and Countess Trenton returned to Salassio from their two-month honeymoon.

"It is so good to be home at last. Not that our honeymoon was not something to be treasured, my love." Archie squeezed his wife's hand as they entered his Bellstrand townhouse.

"No offense taken, dear. I agree, it is good to be home. The first thing I require is a hot bath and at least three days' sleep. If you will excuse me, I will go upstairs and get things underway."

"Of course, dearest." He watched her ascend the main staircase.

"My lord." His butler approached.

"Stephens. It is good to see you, old man. Any disasters while we were away?"

Stephens was a loyal but a dispassionate man. One day was as monotonous as the next. Rise, do your duties, and rest. Care for little and repeat accordingly. Routine was his friend and family. Favorite color, gray.

"Everything is running smoothly as intended, my lord." He took Archie's hat and coat. "There is quite a bit of correspondence awaiting you in your study, my lord."

Archie headed directly for the study. He knew there were a few matters that were anxiously awaiting his attention. In particular, his business dealings with George Hastings, his new brother-in-law.

Among the stack of invitations and donation requests there were a number of messages from his man-of-business. Daniel Crossings was not one to mince words. He got right to the point with lethal precision and accuracy. Archie chose to open the most recent missive first. It contained eight words: "You are practically destitute. We need to talk."

Panic hit Archie as he continued to sift through the pile, finding a missive from George dated almost a month ago.

"Temison has called our marker. I have settled our debt but will require you reimburse me for half the call amount. Contact me upon your return. Walsenburg."

This was not possible. There must be some kind of error. The ships were all on their way prior to his leaving on his honeymoon. They must have arrived by now. Even if they were delayed, they would have still made port long before now.

He searched the pile for a more recent letter from George confirming the ship's arrival and that everything was back on track. Nothing.

"Stephens!"

The butler came in looking alarmed but impassive. "My lord. Is there anything the matter?"

"Please send word to the countess that I was called away on urgent business. I do not know when I will return."

"Of course, my lord."

"Have my horse brought around immediately."

"The Count of Trenton to see you, my lord." George was almost done with his late morning tea when Dobbs interrupted his peace. "I asked he await you in your study."

"Good man, Dobbs. I shall be in directly."

George finished his tea, folded his paper carefully, and made his way to the study.

"Where the hell have you been?" George almost screamed the words as he stormed into the study and loudly slammed the door.

"Is that a riddle?" Archie followed him with his eyes as he took the chair behind his desk. "Where the hell do you think I have been? On my honeymoon as you are very well aware." He took one of the two empty chairs in front of the marquess's desk. "What has been happening since I have been away?"

George looked at him in apparent disbelief. "Oh. Not very much. My mother was abducted, forced into a scandalous and inferior marriage, assumed the title of an obscure Artemisian barony and, let me see, what else has happened?" George mockingly looked around as if trying to remember. "Oh yes! We are RUINED!"

Archie leaned back in his chair. "It cannot be as bad as all that, George. We will get to your mother's situations in a moment. How are you defining ruined?"

"Ruined? Derelict, tumbled down, broke, at sixes and sevens, destitute, paupers? You know? It is when you have nothing left and are at the mercy of the elements and the law. Ruined!"

"Am I to surmise the ships did not come in?"

"You surmise correctly. They were taken hostage by pirates. I paid the requested ransom, but the ships were not released as promised."

"Where are they now?"

"They may have been scuttled for all we know."

Archie sat there completely dumbfounded. "Can we confirm that? Is there no chance of our recovering the ships or at least their cargo?"

"Even if we had the will and the way, we do not possess the

resources. We were overextended as it was. Add to that the amount of the ransom and the loss in revenue and we are deeply in debt."

"Let us think for a moment." Archie stood and began to pace. "I can pull together fifty thousand in local currency if necessary."

"Your half of what is already owed will take up most of that." George was looking straight out the window as if seeing the angel of death beckoning to him from the garden.

"What of your family? They will help, will they not?"

"My mother may be willing, but her new husband will not be as easily swayed." He turned toward Archie leaning on his arms, into his desk. "There was a moment there when she had been abducted without a trace that I thought we might have a chance." George sat back and smiled a wicked smile. "If she had been found dead, I would have inherited all that is hers, and we would have been able to place all this ugliness behind us."

"So, what happened?" Archie sat back down.

"She was rescued by Mr. Thomas Smyth, drifter."

"So, she was rescued. She is still a very wealthy woman and a doting mother. She will give you anything you want. All you have ever had to do was ask."

"If only it were that simple." George walked over to the bar and poured himself a large glass of brandy.

"It is a bit early for spirits, is it not, old man?" Archie became more concerned to see George Hastings, sixth Marquess of Walsenburg and staunch stickler for propriety and societal mores, having a drink before noon. These were desperate times indeed.

"It is much later than you think, my friend." George downed the entire contents of the glass and filled it once more. "How rude of me." He turned to face Archie. "May I offer you one?"

Archie simply shook his head, rejecting the offer. "Fine, so we work with what we have." He came to stand by George, taking the still full glass from his grasp. "Who is the new husband and what do we have on him?"

"His name is Thomas Smyth. He materialized in Salassio in early September and has infiltrated the Elite with surgical accuracy." He walked over to one of the two wingback chairs by the fireplace and sat down as if weighing a ton. "He was the one who actually found her in some shack in or around Mariposa. She was apparently so grateful, she agreed to marry him out of some sort of misplaced gratitude."

"That sounds too fantastic to be true. Have you had the story validated?" Archie sat in the empty chair on the other side of the mantel.

"Investigated, dissected, and validated. She married the vagrant."

"All right, but as a widow of a noble she must have rights and authorities over what was hers prior to the marriage, does she not?"

George looked at him and smiled. "You are reaching, my friend. You know as well as I do that as a woman in our society, noble or commoner, she enjoys very few rights."

"But widows have always…"

"Ah but she is no longer a widow, now is she?" George almost laughed seeing Archie revisit all the alternatives he had already considered and discarded multiple times.

"What of the mysterious Mr. Thomas Smyth? Have you investigated him personally?"

"I have. Apparently, he does not exist. At least not prior to his appearance in Salassio last month."

"And you do not find that curious?"

George snapped. "Of course I find it curious, you idiot!" He tried to relax once again. "Curious or not we cannot find proof of anything. We have nothing to hold over his head or enough ammunition to force his hand."

They sat in silence for some time. "I hate to say it, but it seems we have but one option left to us." Archie gave George a deliberate look, knowing they were both thinking the same thing. "Mr. Smyth must be made to disappear. Permanently." But how?

CHAPTER THIRTY-THREE

Remote location on the outskirts of the kingdom

Teddy heard the hoofbeats from half a mile away. The cottage was perfectly located. It was easily defendable but with three escape routes in the event one needed a quick getaway. Visibility was mostly downhill with a 360-degree view of the countryside.

The cottage itself was spacious. It had three sleeping chambers and a small but functional kitchen with what was once a bountiful garden.

Teddy had been camped out here for a month. He used it as a central command of sorts, supporting Thomas as best he could, considering the remoteness of the location and the challenges of movement and scarcity of resources.

He heard the rider dismount in front of the building and walk the few steps to the front door. "Who goes there?" Standing to the left of the door with a pistol in hand, he waited for a response.

"Beelzebub. Who were you expecting?" the familiar voice responded with sarcasm.

Teddy opened the door still pointing the pistol at the newcomer. "I could have shot you, you know?"

"I am well aware of the danger I have placed myself in, my nervous little friend." Thomas walked in as if he was entering his own home. "I also know what an excellent shot you are. You would never aim to kill unless you knew it was necessary."

Placing the pistol back in his waistband, Teddy closed the door.

"What news?" Thomas sat down at the only table in the room. There were three other wooden chairs but very little else. Teddy used one of the bedrooms for himself. Another was reserved for late-night visitors needing a place to rest, with the third utilized as storage and security.

"Trenton is back from his honeymoon. He wasted no time in meeting with the marquess. Our sources tell us he looked visibly ill as he left Miramarea Abbey."

"I can only guess the marquess has told him they are in deep financial trouble. How much are they bleeding?" Thomas could speculate but he preferred the facts.

"Over one hundred thousand if the reports can be trusted. With Walsenburg's inability to transfer the Gables acreage to Tenison, the debt looms and grows.

"They do not have many alternatives. If Trenton liquidates all of his unentailed assets, he can likely come up with sixty thousand at most. Walsenburg has nothing left he can sell. Everything he has left is entailed as part of the marquisate. What few friends he has do not have those sums in fluid capital available, and if they did, I cannot see them offering them to His Lordship. That leaves only the dowager marchioness."

Thomas liked what he was hearing. "I have that road covered and barricaded. The baroness cannot offer her son a penny without my consent. Besides, the weak-chinned lordling would never approach her with the truth. He would likely spin some sort of business opportunity too good to ignore. What of Tenison?"

"He is still holding on to the three stolen ships and their cargo. He is desperate to divest himself of the whole lot but has encountered insurmountable obstacles at every turn."

"Good. Keep him cornered. We will deal with him in our own good time."

"Every other detail is under control and on schedule." Teddy had one more piece of information to share but was unsure how to approach it. "There is one more thing."

"Out with it."

"The baroness paid an impromptu visit on Mr. Miles Granger. They spent most of the day going over the barony's accounts. She was not happy with your spending ways."

Thomas laughed. "That little minx. Defying me when I am not around."

"In point of fact, she really has not defied you. You never actually told her she could not meet with Granger or review the accounts, now did you?"

"You have a point." He shrugged it off. "It is of little consequence. She can do nothing to stop me or hinder my plans."

"What is our next move?" As if he didn't know.

"We now go on the defensive for a while." Thomas poured himself a glass of brandy. Teddy had little food, but he was well supplied with quality spirits. "We have left our two little dandies with only one logical alternative; they must get rid of me." He was now thinking out loud. "Their first attempt will be bribery. When that fails, they will try extortion. As an act of desperation, they will finally resort to murder."

"With the first two they risk exposure."

"They would never confront me themselves. They do not have the stones." He thought carefully. "A seemingly disinterested third party will be recruited for the task." He turned to Teddy and smiled. "Beware of Greeks bearing gifts, my friend."

"Are we to be on the lookout for Greeks now?"

"More like a weak impersonation of one."

CHAPTER THIRTY-FOUR

Dunnfee Court, Artemisia

Thomas was finishing his morning meal when Analisa stormed into the dining room. "Thomas." She fixed him with a steely stare. "We need to talk."

He'd been expecting this confrontation. "Regarding what exactly?"

"Will you please explain these exorbitant expenses of yours in the past month?"

"I will not." He put his utensils down and slowly wiped his mouth. "And you are violating our agreement."

"I beg to differ, sir. I agreed to never contradict or disagree with your decisions in public. However, I reserve the right to challenge you privately. I exercise that privilege now. What are these expenses relating to?"

He stood and slowly walked over to her. Three inches from nose to nose. "As your husband and in my capacity as Baron Pennington, I will do as I please, when I please, and as often as I please and there is NOTHING you can do to stop me. Moreover, I owe you no explanation. Ask me again and you will receive the same response." He walked past her, slightly grazing her shoulder with his arm. "Do you feel better now, my love?" He disappeared through the door.

Analisa had not said five words to him in the past eight days. They still took their morning and evening meals together, but now they all came with a chilly reception. He had attempted multiple conversations with her on several occasions but always met with monosyllabic responses or none at all.

The knock at the door broke his concentration. "Enter."

"Pardon the intrusion, my lord. There is a Mr. James Crossings to see you."

Thomas looked up from the documents he'd been reviewing. "Did he state his purpose, Mr. Powers?"

"He refuses to divulge the purpose of his visit, my lord. He insists it is urgent and in your best interest to hear him out."

Thomas grinned. He'd been expecting this visit. *Round one begins.* "I will receive him in the stables in thirty minutes."

Powers looked surprised and a little shocked. "The stables, my lord?"

"The stables is what I said, did I not?"

"Yes of course, my lord. I will have him escorted to the stables in thirty minutes as instructed."

If this was the visit he was expecting, he wanted to put the messenger as ill at ease as possible. The privy would have been perfect, but the stables would have to do.

Thirty minutes later a footman entered the stables followed closely by a tall young man who looked to be in his late teens or early twenties. He looked nervous but you could easily tell he was streetwise. His attire was common, but his eyes were very sharp.

"My lord, Mr. James Crossings to see you."

Thomas was brushing down his new mount and didn't bother to acknowledge his guest.

James stood patiently and waited to be recognized. This was nothing new to him. He was of the working class and routinely ignored by the upper classes.

"James Crossings." Thomas finally said his name out loud. "Have we met?"

"Not that I can remember, my lord."

The boy had confidence. You had to admire that quality in a man, of any age. "What can I do for you, James Crossings? Please do not waste my time. I am a very busy man."

"As you wish, my lord." No cowering. Impressive. "I have been instructed to present you with an offer my employer believes you will appreciate."

"I am all ears, sir. Please go on."

"The particulars are all written down here." James presented him with a sealed document. "My employer instructed I wait for a response."

Thomas broke the seal and read the letter. He made James wait for his response and his reaction for several long seconds.

He gave a burst of laughter, spooking several of the horses, but not James. "Your employer is expecting a response to this insulting offer?"

"He is indeed, my lord. What shall I convey back to him?"

"Tell him if his offer was twice the amount and then twice that amount, I would never agree to their conditions." He threw the letter at James's feet.

James picked it up, refolded it, and bowed. "I will relay the message, my lord." He turned.

"James Crossings!" Thomas bellowed. "How old are you?"

James turned back to face Thomas. "Nineteen, my lord."

Thomas assessed the young man, closely looking for a weakness. A flaw. "Tell me what scares you, James Crossings."

"Hopelessness, my lord."

"Not poverty, incarceration…death?"

"All are lifelong and constant companions, my lord. I keep their inevitability close, for their constant threat keeps me focused." James could see Thomas was expecting more. "It is not the threat of death that destroys, it is the lack of hope. I have been working my entire life to be better than I am. Better than my station in life. Yet it is my station and the challenges of that circumstance that drive me to be better than I am. But I cannot allow or afford myself the luxury of losing hope. If hope is taken from you…?" He didn't continue. He simply stared at Thomas awaiting a condescending dismissal.

"That is quite a virtuous philosophy for life, James Crossings. I do not believe I have ever been in the presence of someone as pious as yourself."

"Pious, my lord? I am the lowest of the low. My presence here today confirms that fact. But I do what I must to survive. I have those who depend on me, and someone must always be sacrificed. In my case, I chose to sacrifice myself. It is as simple as that." Again, he awaited a dismissal. When one was not offered, he volunteered. "Is that all, my lord?"

"Yes, that will be all, James Crossings. Do not forget to convey my response to your employer. If you will include the insulting sarcasm, I would be most grateful."

"I will do my best, my lord."

CHAPTER THIRTY-FIVE

Capital city of Salassio, Sonastare

"What exactly did he say?" George was discussing the results of his and Trenton's offer to Thomas Smyth. He, Archie, and Daniel had met at The Emperor's Den to discuss strategies.

"He said your offer was insultingly unacceptable. He would not agree to your terms at ten times the amount offered." Daniel had sent his younger brother James as envoy. With Thomas Smyth a nobody, the chances of tracing the message back to him and to the two lords were remote. Of course, who else but these two greedy bastards would benefit from Mr. Smyth's removal? But as with everything, it is not what you know but what you can prove. He did not expect his brother to be so stupid as to give his real name upon meeting the baron.

"Well, we are certainly not going to offer more." George looked disappointed but not surprised.

"Do we have any leverage on this man at all? He must have a few dark secrets buried somewhere," Archie asked for the hundredth time in a week.

"We have been digging into his past for the last six weeks. There is no trace of a Thomas Smyth anywhere in the two kingdoms or abroad until he arrived on our shores.

"The name is obviously false but there is nothing linking him to anything or anyone under Smyth or any other name. We simply have nothing to work with."

"Very well then. We will go with our original plan." George hated to resort to deadly violence, but he was desperate and could see no other way out.

"What do you mean no?" Daniel was walking quickly to catch up with James.

"Exactly what I said. No. I will not take a life under any circumstance except to save the lives of me or mine."

"Jamie, the man is a scoundrel and a thief. He forced Lady Analisa into marriage and is stealing her money as we speak. His name is not even Thomas Smyth. We do not know who he is." He grabbed James by the shoulder and spun him around to face him. "He is probably a killer. You would be doing the world a favor and saving countless lives in the process." He smiled. "Besides, we are being paid a pretty penny for providing this life-saving service to humanity. Come on, what do you say?"

"I say no."

"Very well. I will find someone else to do the job, but you will not benefit a penny from the proceeds. You mark my words, James Robert Crossings. Not a single penny." By then James was out of earshot.

CHAPTER THIRTY-SIX

Remote location on the outskirts of the kingdom

Three men stood when Thomas strolled into the cottage. Teddy had sent word to meet him there that night for an update.

The three present were known to him, but Teddy was their handler and he was late.

"Good evening, gentlemen. I understand you have news."

"We do indeed, sir." The taller of the three took a military step forward. He seemed uncertain as to what he was allowed to share directly with Thomas. Few had ever met Thomas face-to-face. They all worked behind the scenes in a compartmentalized structure. Everyone knew someone, but no one knew everyone, with the exception of Thomas himself. As the organization's leader, he was the only one of the group privy to every detail of the operation.

The organization was obviously large and complex, but only Thomas knew the extent of it completely.

"Please stand at ease, gents. Sit down if you would rather. I assume you have come straight from Salassio. It is a long journey and you must be exhausted."

They all looked at each other as if they were unsure what to do.

The sounds of footsteps just outside the front door placed them all on alert.

"My apologies for my tardiness, gentlemen." Teddy came marching in as if just off the parade grounds at royal court.

"I hope she was worth keeping us waiting." Thomas gave him the once-over, noting his fresh and clean-shaven appearance and fashionable attire.

"She certainly was, but not for the reasons you may be thinking." Teddy placed his pistols and dagger on the table. Looking at his companions, "Have you shared your news with Thomas?"

"Not yet, Mr. Millbar. We were waiting for you."

"Go on then. Speak freely." Teddy pulled up one of the older chairs from the side wall.

"Word has spread an assassin is wanted for a very covert assignment." The tall visitor continued. "No one knows the specifics, but stealth and anonymity are required. No street thug need apply."

"Chase here met with a Mr. Cousins at the Pick and Poke on Dairy last week." He motioned to Chase to take up the story from there.

"We met in shadows where this Mr. Cousins offered me six hundred in local currency to assassinate a dangerous thief and potential murderer threatening the crown.

"No name was given but the location was Dunnfee Court and the description fit you to a hair, sir."

"Just as we suspected." Thomas brought over the brandy and five glasses. Sitting down in the empty chair, he poured each a drink. "Go on, Chase."

"Wait a moment," Teddy interrupted. "I thought their next step would be extortion. Are they going off script?"

"Not necessarily. I had assumed they were forced to skip extortion having nothing to leverage their threat against." Thomas looked at Teddy as if expecting him to understand. "Do you not see? This tells us two important things. First, they have very limited resources. If they were more sophisticated with deeper pockets, they would have found the ammunition we left for them in Paris and Madrid."

"Agreed." Teddy was beginning to see where this was heading.

"The second thing this provides is confirmation of what we have suspected all along."

"They are a bunch of idiots," they all seemed to chorus at once.

Thomas sat back with a satisfied grin. "Exactly."

"All right, so we are skipping over extortion and going straight to murder. Are we prepared for this?"

"The escalation is not the problem. We have always expected this as their only recourse. We essentially drove them to it." He stood and walked to the window, glass in hand, deep in thought. "No, our concern is a sloppy execution. Stupidity breeds carelessness. Carelessness breeds desperation and fear. There is where the danger lies."

He suddenly turned toward the group. "Gentlemen, we must help them. We must make sure they are afforded every opportunity and resource in planning the perfect murder."

"That is very generous of you, Thomas. I volunteer to kill you myself if it will help." Teddy picked up one of the pistols he'd discarded on the table when he entered. "I am ready now if you are amiable to the idea?"

The three newcomers looked as if they'd missed something important.

"He jests, gents." Thomas kept his eyes fixed on Teddy who slowly lowered his pistol still in his grip. "Of course I do not mean to carry out the murder, simply to help them plan it safely, keepiing us in total control."

"This is why you do not have any friends." Teddy put the pistol back on the table.

"I resent that remark. I have many friends. Willing to die for me if necessary."

"Name two." Teddy crossed his arms over his chest in sarcastic anticipation.

"Alexander." No reaction. "And you."

Teddy emptied his glass and slammed it on the table. "Get on with it then. I am actually looking forward to planning your death. I hope it is painful and bloody." He winked. "Figuratively speaking of course."

"Fine. The first thing we need to do is make things easier for them. Coordinating a murder at Dunnfee Court from Salassio is challenging at best. I will plan on returning to Salassio, where they can have easy access.

"My wife's daughter has returned from her honeymoon. The baroness is anxious to spend time with her. This presents us with a perfect excuse for returning to the island.

"Now as for the details of my demise."

CHAPTER THIRTY-SEVEN

Capital city of Salassio, Sonastare

This was getting old. George detested these trips to the Emperor's Den. He was a marquess. Born to the kingdom's Elite. It was his destiny and his birthright to enjoy the advantages of affluence and privilege.

Here he was, yet again, with these miscreants, secretly plotting crimes and misdeeds for the sake of maintaining what was his by birth. Intolerable.

"Have we secured an agent for the deed?" He had lost his patience with Daniel long ago. The man seemed to take twice as much time as necessary to accomplish the simplest of tasks.

"We have, my lord." Daniel leaned in so as not to be overheard. Since they were alone in the pub's private dining room, the dangers of that were remote at best. "He has agreed to the deed but is demanding additional funds."

George looked at Archie and back at Daniel. "How much more?"

"Double the amount, my lord." Daniel looked around as if planning the overthrow of the kingdom. "In return, he will work out the details of the assassination. He guarantees it will go unchallenged. If investigated, it will appear as a tragic accident and nothing more."

"Pay the man." Archie wanted this done and over with quickly. He'd been selling off what assets he could without notice.

"I will confirm his commitment, my lord. He will leave for Dunnfee Court immediately." Daniel made to leave. George grabbed his arm.

"No need to travel south. The baron and baroness are planning a trip to Salassio in the very near future. With my sister's recent return, my mother wishes to spend some time with her before they are both overwhelmed by the demands of their respective duties."

"Do you know when they will be arriving and how long they plan on staying?" Daniel was grateful for the baron's consideration, but altering his plans with minimal notice was never appreciated.

"I have not received an itinerary. But they will send word as soon as the details are finalized." He looked to Archie. "Has my sister received word?"

"Not that she has shared with me." It was like being caught in a whirlwind. "I assume they will stay at your home while on the island. My townhouse is inadequate for the task."

"No need. In recognition of her new title, the crown has seen fit to restore her status as an Elite. She and her baron will take up residence at Serenity Hall for the duration of their stay on Bellstrand." Only his mother could find a way of turning a bad situation completely in her favor.

"I will update our friend." Daniel stood with one last look for any last-minute changes. Seeing none, he bowed. "My lords."

Joseline came thundering into his study minutes after his arrival home. "This cannot be true." She was looking at him as if he was supposed to know what she was talking about.

"Good day, Joseline. To what are you referring and why can it not be true?"

"You are pleading ignorance of the facts?" She was livid.

"I plead ignorance of the subject at hand." Now his temper was being tested. "What the hell are you talking about, woman?"

"I was just informed the Baron and Baroness of Pennington will be taking up residence at Serenity Hall." She slammed the door to his study, stormed to one of the empty chairs facing his desk, and dropped like a sack of wheat. "I will not allow it, do you hear me, George? I will absolutely not permit that disreputable couple to sully the pristine order of this glorious island."

As if she had the power to do anything about the matter. But why not humor her a brief second. It may prove entertaining, he thought.

"And just what do you intend on doing about it, my dear?" He was not even looking in her direction.

"I will file a grievance with the crown. They have no right to change the rules of society without justification. We are the Elite in Sonastare, and we should have a say. It is we who will be living with these people. It is our lives that are being turned upside down. Where is their consideration for us?"

George turned slowly to look at her outraged countenance. Was it her condition that had her so emotionally unstable or had she always been irrationally illogical and he had simply refused to recognize it?

"Listen to me carefully, Joseline. I realize you are overtaxed due to your increasing condition, so I will overlook your disrespectful behavior just this once out of compassion. But raise your voice to me again, and I will exile you to Treadstone. Am I making myself clear?"

Joseline knew she had made a mistake in confronting George in this manner. It was true her condition had taken control of her emotions, but she should have known better. Why wouldn't that woman simply fade away? This was all her fault.

"Bellstrand belongs to the crown. We live here under their protection and thanks to their generosity. They have every right to implement, eradicate, or alter any rule, law, or standard they see fit, without the slightest regard for how you or any other resident of this island will feel or how you will react. You have no say. You have no voice. YOU HAVE NO RIGHTS!" The last he shouted loudly enough to be heard by the staff passing by his study.

"But George. You must…"

He settled back into his chair, looking up at the ceiling. "Maybe it was a mistake marrying you as my parents suggested."

"They were opposed to the marriage? But I am the daughter of the Duke and Duchess of Dials. You were and are fortunate to have me by your side. I am providing you and the marquisate with an heir. How dare you? How dare they?"

"Be gone, Joseline. I do not wish to set eyes on you."

Joseline stood, making every effort to maintain her pride as she did so. Tears covered her cheeks as she reached the door. How dare anyone besmirch her person or her family name. That woman was to blame for all of this. With or without George's support, she would do something about this injustice. She was done taking a back seat to that hag.

"Dobbs!" she was screeching as she barreled through the majestic halls of Miramarea Abbey. "Dobbs! Where is that man? He is never where he is supposed to be."

Dobbs appeared at the end of the hall as she approached the main staircase. "You called, my lady?"

"There you are. Have Marissa brought to me in my sitting room immediately."

"Certainly, my lady."

Twenty minutes later, a nervous Merissa Jonas stood before the mistress of the house. "You asked for me, my lady?"

"I did indeed." Joseline waved to the empty chair to her right. "Have a seat, my dear."

Marissa took a seat but stayed on the edge, uncertain of her fate.

"Are you happy here, Marissa? Have you been treated well?"

In point of fact, working at Miramarea Abbey was a less than pleasant experience. The marquess and marchioness were selfish, self-centered, insensitive, overbearing, unrealistic, and unfair tyrants. She had only been with the family for four months but had come to despise and fear them within a week of being here. But Marissa had a mother and a younger sister to support. Marrying well was not an option for her considering her humble beginnings and a nonexistent dowry.

"Oh yes, my lady. I am quite happy here."

Joseline didn't truly believe her. She was aware of Marissa's circumstances. Sadly, the last few years had seen a significant turnover in the staff at Miramarea Abbey and most of the marquisate's other residences. It was becoming more and more difficult to keep retainers until Joseline resorted to extortion. Most of her current staff was, to some degree, forced to maintain their positions for fear of being ruined by the Marchioness of Walsenburg. Marissa was no exception.

"That is very good, my dear. You see, I have a little mission for you." Joseline smiled while Marissa cringed. "As you may have heard, the Baron and Baroness of Pennington are due to take up residence at Serenity Hall very soon. They have a limited staff and will need our help to reestablish themselves on Bellstrand, as it were."

"Certainly, my lady. Anything we can do to help the baron and baroness in their transition will be our pleasure." Marissa was still dubious of the ulterior motives behind this odd meeting.

"I will be sending you along with a few other retainers to assist the happy couple when they arrive. I need for you to go above and beyond your duties as housemaid." Joseline gave Marissa a sidelong look, hoping she understood what was expected of her.

"I will be happy to do whatever I can to help, my lady."

"That is very good of you, Marissa. I will give you further instructions when the time comes." She took up her teacup. "That is all for now." The audience was at an end.

Marissa rose, dipped a quick curtsy, and quickly left the room.

CHAPTER THIRTY-EIGHT

They were just a few hours outside of Salassio. Their five-day journey had felt even longer considering Analisa's continued silence throughout the trip.

Since his ultimatum, Thomas could count on both hands the number of words she'd directed his way. She was hurt, and she was very angry, but mostly, she was frustrated with the situation. He had not been necessarily unkind since he'd forced her into this devil's bargain. In fact, he had neither asked nor expected anything of her, giving her free reign over all but her finances.

The household accounts were an exception as well as her pin money. None of which were given limits or restrictions. Or at least, none that she'd been made aware of. She was certain Mr. Granger was keeping Thomas informed of every penny she spent, where and how much.

"I wanted to thank you for allowing this trip to Salassio. Evelyn has written me endless letters requesting my return to Bellstrand for a visit or permission for her to come out and see me at Dunnfee Court. This way, I will not only have the opportunity of spending time with my children, but with my dear friends as well."

"Not at all, my dear. I know how much you love your children and your friends." He checked for any signs of a thaw.

A little more than two hours later, they were boarding the ferry taking them to Bellstrand island and her family.

"Good afternoon, my lady." Cornelius DelStar, Chief Steward, greeted her with deference. "It is good to have you back with us."

He turned more formally to address Thomas. "Welcome back to Bellstrand, Baron Pennington. I hope your journey was a pleasant one."

"All journeys seem arduous these days, DelStar."

"I am sorry for any difficulties, my lord." He ushered them aboard and onto the main deck. "Your personal effects have not yet arrived, but they will be forwarded to Serenity Hall as soon as they do. Your coach will be transported over with you on this ferry. I was informed the manor has been fully stocked and your household domestics will be to full staffing by the conclusion of the week."

"Thank you, Mr. DelStar. Efficient as always. We are so fortunate to have you with us."

"The honor is mine, my lady."

He left them to find their comfort for the short trip across.

The entire trip, Thomas had been vigilant, watching for any attempts on his life. He didn't really expect any. Chase had accepted the contract on his life and had coordinated an elaborate plan to assassinate the baron, making it look like an accident. All the players were set and the particulars had been ironed out, but there were always the elements of desperation and stupidity one had to contend with.

"Baron and Baroness Pennington." They both turned to find Tenison approaching them from the main entrance. "I am not sure you would remember me, Reardon Tenison, Viscount Abernathy at your service." He gave them a tenuous bow.

Thomas had not been formally introduced to the viscount but he certainly knew who he was. Maybe even better than Tenison himself.

"Good day, my lord. It is very nice to see you again." Analisa gave him a welcoming smile. "Would you care to join us?"

"Regrettably, my lady, I have guests on the lower deck who await me. I saw you board and could not resist the opportunity of being one of the first to welcome you back home."

"So very kind of you, my lord. We are over the moon with the joy of seeing all of our family and friends after such a long absence."

"Well, I must be off. Please do not hesitate to call on me if there is anything I can do for you while you are on Bellstrand." Another curt bow and off he went.

The rat. Thomas was certain he'd planned this "accidental encounter" to make sure he could confirm their return to the island.

The crossing was pleasant if not fast enough for Analisa's taste. She was anxious to get home and see her daughter, now a married woman and probably in the family way.

Joseline was also further along, and she wanted to see how she was progressing prior to her upcoming confinement.

It took a few minutes for their coach to be unloaded and the team properly harnessed.

Within the hour, they were on their way to Serenity Hall. Luggage to follow.

They rode into the manor's courtyard. She immediately recognized one of her under-butlers, Francis Pitts, waiting at the portico to greet them.

There was no point in having Powers make this long trip, particularly at his age, for only a few weeks' time. He stayed behind at Dunnfee Court along with most of her long-term retainers. Only Tully and Bruce travelled with them as was proper.

When the coach came to a complete stop, a footman immediately opened the door and dropped the step, allowing them to alight.

Thomas exited first and assisted Analisa down. Pitts came to join them. "Welcome home, my lord, my lady. Was it an agreeable crossing?"

"Good day, Pitts. We could not arrive fast enough for my taste if I were being honest."

"I can certainly understand the sentiment, my lady." The group began walking toward the house as Pitts brought them both up to date on recent goings-on.

"Countess Trenton sent word she would like for you to join her and the count for dinner this evening if you are not too tired. She has also invited the Duke and Duchess of Welby, the Marquess and Marchioness of Walsenburg, Viscount and Viscountess Cross, as well as Baron and Baroness Kelt. I cannot say if everyone has confirmed, only that the invitations were extended.

"You are both expected at seven o'clock sharp. But if you would prefer to stay home this evening, I will have Cook prepare a late supper at your convenience."

Analisa looked to Thomas, who seemed to be surveying the area as if looking for something well hidden.

"Do you have any objections to our joining our family and friends for dinner this evening, my lord?"

"I have no objections although we should not stay late. We need our rest after the ordeal of the past few days."

Not a ringing endorsement but not a rejection either. She would take it.

CHAPTER THIRTY-NINE

They arrived at the local residence of the Count and Countess of Trenton promptly at seven that evening. The walk and portico were brightly lit. The foliage was still green but without blossoms. It was much too late in the year.

Leaving the coach and coachman to their tasks, Baron and Baroness Pennington made the short walk to the front door. The door seemed to mysteriously open as they approached, revealing a very severe-looking butler. Just behind him came a tidal wave of women. It appeared as if the poor man would be enveloped.

"Good evening, my lord and my lady." Stephens began his familiar opening salvo.

"No need, Stephens." Marie had now overtaken the poor man and was halfway down the steps.

"We will take it from here." Maggie waved Stephens away as if shooing a fly. "What took you so long? You live fifteen minutes away for heaven's sake."

Ana felt like laughing. These were some of the highest-ranking matriarchs in Sonastarian society. Never a word or hair out of place. They set the standards, fashions, and trends. But put them together and they were fifteen again.

She decided to have a little fun. "Good evening, ladies." She gave them all a little curtsy. "It is delightful to see you again. It has been an age. I hope you are enjoying this evening's mild weather. It is predicted to turn quite frosty within the next few weeks."

They all looked at each other in confusion. Ada was the last to arrive but the first to voice her concerns. "Have you suffered some sort of head injury?" She looked from Ana to Thomas, leaned in, and whispered, "Has he struck you?"

Now Ana did actually laugh. She, too, disregarded all sense of propriety and reached out to take Ada in her arms, kissing her on both cheeks. "I am perfectly fine, you silly goose. I was simply having a little fun at your expense."

They all entered the foyer, leaving the world outside. Hugs, kisses, and giggling ensued as Thomas waited patiently by Stephens, who was to escort and announce them formally.

Analisa looked to the two men. *Very well. Let's get this performance over and done.* She leaned into her circle of friends, sisters. "I suggest the three of you go on ahead. We need to make the obligatory entrance."

They all gave a frustrated look. "We would not be wasting time on these antiquated customs were we at my home this evening." All Ada wanted to do was sit in a quiet space with her friends and catch up.

"No one under the age of forty would consider them antiquated, my dear." Maggie linked arms with Marie and Ada and led them back down the hall. "We are simply getting old."

"I beg your pardon?" Ada said, feigning righteous indignation.

"Duchesses do not beg, Your Grace. Please try to keep up."

A few seconds later, Stephens entered the family sitting room. "The Baron and Baroness of Pennington."

Analisa entered, holding on to Thomas's arm. Evelyn came rushing forward. "Oh, Mother, you look wonderful. Marriage must agree with you."

She addressed Thomas more formally. Dipping into a light curtsy, "Good evening, my lord. Welcome to our home."

Ana stepped in as Archie approached to partner his wife. "Count and Countess Trenton, please allow me to introduce you to my husband, Thomas Smyth, Baron Pennington." Archie and Thomas bowed to one another.

"Thank you for the invitation, my lord and lady. Having just arrived on the island, it is a bit overwhelming. Friends and family always have a calming effect."

Evelyn took her mother aside, drawing her toward George and Joseline patiently awaiting their turn. "We invited the Duke and Duchess of Colton to join us, but they are not in residence. I did not think you would be too disappointed."

Analisa was not close with her cousin, so it was not much of a disappointment.

Joseline sat while George rose to greet his mother. "You are looking well, Mother. I hope your trip north was not too taxing."

"Long but comfortable, darling." She kissed both his cheeks. "I am simply happy to be here." Turning to Joseline she smiled broadly. "And how are you feeling, my dear? Any strange cravings?"

As much as Joseline had grown to resent her mother-in-law, she feared the wrath of the powerful ladies present. She smiled as demurely as she could muster. "I am feeling fine, my lady. So far all is proceeding nicely. Doctor Binnicker is very pleased with my progress."

Ana reached out and gently squeezed her hands. "If there is anything you require, you simply must reach out to me." She looked over her shoulder. "You can reach out to any one of these ladies behind me. Not one will hesitate to come to your aid."

Obviously, the harpies had not shared Joseline's cutting remarks with Baroness Pennington. That was an unexpected surprise and an advantage Joseline planned to exploit. "There is something I would like to discuss with you if you would not mind."

Ana came and sat next to Joseline. "Of course, dear. How can I help?"

"There is a lovely young lady working for us by the name of Marissa Jonas. She is one of our upstairs maids and has been an angel for the past few months. The truth is we simply do not have a place for her at this time, but I am reluctant to let her go until I can secure a safe position for her elsewhere. I have offered to have her relocated to one of our other properties, but she does not wish to leave Salassio." She gave Analisa a moment. "Would you be able to find a place for her at Serenity Hall? I realize it is a very unexpected request, so please do not feel obligated."

Without missing a beat, "Not at all, dearest. She is more than welcome. I asked Georgette to remain at Dunnfee Court. I would welcome and appreciate having a reliable young lady around to assist me."

"Oh, how wonderful. I will let Marissa know in the morning. You are very gracious, my lady. Thank you."

"Not another word about it, my dear. It is my pleasure."

Just then dinner was announced, and everyone adjourned to the dining room.

The evening was a great success with everyone enjoying light conversation and the occasional gossip.

"Any word from our friend?" Archie approached George with a brandy. The two were isolated from the rest of the party, standing by the garden windows.

"No details. He has assured me all is as it should be. The situation should be resolved by month end."

"Such a shame making her a widow again so soon." Archie looked over to where Analisa was in a deep conversation with the Duchess of Welby.

"Survival of the fittest, my friend." George took a drink from his glass. "It is either him, or us."

"William has spoken with Aguste on multiple occasions. He has uncovered nothing of value to our efforts." Ada was Ana's biggest advocate and was becoming increasingly frustrated with this "getting nowhere" campaign of theirs.

"I would not be as concerned if I knew when this ordeal was scheduled to end. Unfortunately, he has given no indication of a pending finale."

"Why not allow him to return to Dunnfee Court alone? You can take up permanent residence at Serenity Hall."

"I cannot do that, Ada. I have a responsibility to the barony and to the people it supports. Without me present to keep an eye on things, who knows what he is capable of doing."

"I understand but I am still concerned."

"Concerned about what?" Maggie approached.

"Where are our husbands, pray tell? Did they decide to leave us again?" Ada was looking around but could see no signs of hers or anyone else's husband with the exception of George and Archie by the windows.

"They are still with us. They became bored and decided to engage in a game of billiards rather than 'following us around,' as they put it. Now, what concerns you?"

"Oh, the same thing that concerns us all these days."

"The mysterious Mr. Smyth." Maggie quickly covered her mouth with her hand, embarrassed by her faux pas. "Excuse me, Baron Pennington."

"Baron my uncle Bartee's girdle." Ada lived without filters. As a duchess she did not need any.

Hours passed in blissful peace. "My dear. I believe it is time we returned to Serenity Hall. You need your rest." Thomas seemed relaxed but vigilant all at once.

"Yes of course. Where has the time gone."

They took a few moments to make their rounds. Archie and Evelyn walked them to the door. "How long will you be on the island, Mother?"

"For a fortnight at least, dear. Maybe longer." She looked to Thomas for confirmation.

"It is uncertain at this time, my lady. Let us say we do not yet have a date for departure."

"I am planning a shopping trip to Salassio this week. Would you join me?" Evelyn looked hopeful but uncertain.

"That sounds wonderful, dear. Just let me know when, and I will be sure to make arrangements to join you."

A few moments for hugs, kisses, curtseys, and bows and the baron and his baroness were back in their coach heading home.

"Did you enjoy your evening, my lady?"

"I did indeed, my lord." She turned to him. "Thank you for being so kind to my family and friends. And for your patience. We stayed much longer than I had expected."

A few moments of silence followed before she picked up the conversation once more. "You surprise me, sir. Just as I have you pegged as the worst sort of villain, you do something unexpectedly considerate. Almost kind. I do so wish you would settle on a single character. Hating you and liking you from one moment to another is exhausting."

He had to laugh. "If forced to choose between saint or sinner, I will always choose sinner. Sinners have fewer regrets and all of the fun." He leaned in closer; taking both her hands in his and turning them palm up, he placed a kiss on each wrist. "Lord Claudius at your service, my lady. Never forget that."

She abruptly withdrew her hands. The monster. And up came the icy walls of isolation. The remainder of the short ride was completed in absolute silence.

CHAPTER FORTY

"A coaching accident? Is that really the best we can do?" Thomas was once more strategizing with Teddy at the Lamb's End pub.

"It is not the best we can do, but it is something we can control with a fair amount of ease. If you would like to suggest a more suitable demise for yourself, we are at your command."

"Not at all. I just hate the idea of destroying a brand-new coach. Not to mention my suit. And the danger it places on the team of horses." He looked at Teddy as if expecting him to suddenly present an alternate plan.

"Your lady wife can afford to replace it all." What was Thomas expecting from him?

"Fine, a coaching accident it is. Who is charged with setting me up for the fall?"

"The marquess will seek your advice on a property he is looking to purchase in the eastern slopes. It is a three-hour ride from Salassio with two bridges and the Melinger Precipice in between. You will be killed at some point before you reach His Lordship."

"So, which is it to be—a bridge or the precipice?"

Teddy gave him a sheepish grin. "We want to surprise you." He knew this would not please Thomas, who was the kind of man who wanted to know every single detail in advance, leaving nothing to chance.

"Do not fret. Every contingency has been accounted for. No real harm will come to you." Teddy leaned in. "Trust me. The less you know, the less chances of giving anything away."

Thomas wanted to argue but had to agree with Teddy's assessment of the situation.

Thomas left the Lamb's End full of energy. He had agreed to meet Malcolm Gillam at Folton's for a drink before returning to Bellstrand.

"I will walk the distance to Folton's, Jackson. Get yourself something to eat and meet me there in an hour." His coachman nodded his understanding and they parted ways.

It was a beautiful day. A bit on the cool side but very pleasant for a stroll. As was always the case, Thomas's looks drew stares. Young ladies smiled; mature matrons mentally weighed and measured him as suitable husband material for eligible daughters. Gentlemen nodded as they passed while a few dandies smiled at him as well. Nothing that ever interested Thomas but flattering, nevertheless.

He arrived at Folton's, and his hat and coat were collected by a footman who then escorted him to where Malcolm sat with Barns Braiard in casual conversation.

"Good day, gentlemen. How are you both faring this fine afternoon?"

Both gentlemen stood in greeting.

"Not as well as you, if the stories are even remotely to be believed." Braiard gave him a knowing wink as they all took a seat and ordered another round of drinks.

"And just what rumors would those be?"

"Nothing of significant note, *Baron Pennington*." Malcolm felt

Braiard had overstepped and tried to neutralize the rude comment before the offence took root.

"What can I say, gentlemen, we fell in love. It was not planned but it happens."

Malcolm hesitated for a moment. "Rumor also has it the Marquess of Walsenburg is not very happy about the entire situation." He and Barns looked to Thomas for clarification. Nothing.

"He was apparently counting on his mother's good nature to help him out of a financial difficulty, and you are standing in his way," Braiard added, not sure how the information would be received.

"We were with the marquess only two nights ago. He mentioned nothing of needing financial assistance. I believe you are mistaken."

From there the conversation turned to matters of politics and scandal. Business opportunities were also discussed as well as the significance of an Artemisian barony under the control of a Sonastarian Elite. The opportunities and possibilities were endless.

An hour and a half later, Thomas exited the club into his awaiting coach. On the rear-facing seat, he found a folded piece of paper.

Opening it carefully he read the few words it contained:

"*Watch yourself, Danger!*
Hopeless"

CHAPTER FORTY-ONE

"**G**ood morning, Mother." Evelyn strolled into her mother's east gardens at Serenity Hall, just as the sun was rising over the pines, bringing with it some much welcomed warmth.

"Good day, dear." Analisa loved her daughter's visits. She was making it a habit of visiting her mother every morning since she arrived on the island.

"Have you heard? Her Grace is hosting an end of season picnic at Palacio DiSanto at the end of the week. It seems she has invited the entire island and half of Salassio to attend." Together they continued a casual stroll down the main path of the majestic gardens. "Is it not exciting?"

"Ada does have a flair for taking advantage of any situation. We only have a couple of weeks left in the season when the weather will prove cooperative. William has several bills before parliament and needs to secure the support of several nobles who remain undecided. The picnic is to soften them up." Analisa put her arm around her daughter. "But let us not let the ugly realities of life mar what promises to be a spectacular event."

Evelyn, much like George, was not comfortable with these displays of affection. She was simply more tolerant and was always willing to give her mother much more latitude than her older more reserved brother.

"Will you and the baron be attending?" Evelyn turned to her with pleading eyes. "Please say you will. All your friends will be there."

Analisa laughed. "Not only will we be present, but I am assisting Ada with many of the arrangements. She has requested we use our newly found fame to bridge a few of the gaps in negotiations."

"I do not know what half of that meant but I am elated you will be there." Evelyn looked toward the house. "Who is the new maid?"

"Her name is Marissa Jonas. And our Joseline highly recommends her. Is there an issue I need to address?"

"Oh no. She is very pretty and seems quite competent. I simply saw her as a little young to be executing the duties of housekeeper."

"Well, Mrs. Powers felt the girl could use some training as she is only with us for a short while. Joseline is looking for a more permanent position for her, and increasing her domestic skills is always an advantage when competing for a position."

"Just so. Who knows, I may be the one to hire Ms. Jonas if everything goes to plan."

"Goes to what type of plan, dearest?" Analisa looked more closely at her daughter. Her face was fuller and literally glowing. She had been more affectionate of late and more welcoming of her mother's endearing affections. "Oh, my goodness! You are with child, are you not?"

Evelyn broke into tears and a broad smile. "It would appear so, Mother. I have missed my courses in the past two months. I seem to have an unquenchable appetite and my emotions are completely unpredictable."

"Have you been examined by a doctor?"

"No, but Doctor Binnicker is scheduled to come by for a visit this afternoon." More tears. "As soon as he confirms what I feel in my heart to be the case, we will tell the world. Until then, please let us keep this just between the two of us. Even Archie is not yet aware of my condition."

"You have my word, my darling." Analisa took her daughter in her arms and squeezed as if infusing her with all the love she felt would make her explode if not shared. "I am here if and when you need me."

Evelyn broke the embrace. "I need to be on my way. I am meeting Archie for a stroll in the park at ten this morning and I do not wish to be late,"

Analisa reached up and ran her fingers along her daughter's cheek. "Run along, my love. I look forward to a grand announcement very soon."

The noon meal was about to be served when Thomas entered the dining room, dressed in one of his new outfits. He looked very handsome in dark blue, but then, he looked very handsome in anything he wore.

"Have you spoken with the Duchess of Welby?" He asked Analisa as a way to open a dialog. "Apparently, Their Graces are asking for our support during this impromptu picnic of theirs three days hence."

"I have spoken with Ada. William is presenting several bills before parliament and needs additional support to have them adopted. Most or all either directly or indirectly affect trade among the twin kingdoms as well as the Mediterranean island of Milagros. Considering our title, we are in a unique position to assist him in pursuing his endeavors."

Thomas could see many advantages to not only improving trade conditions between the kingdoms, but in making additional contacts among the ruling class of Sonastare. He may be able to gather more information regarding the marquess and his plans in the eastern kingdom.

"What exactly is in it for me, my dear?" Crude but in character.

"For you personally, not a thing with the exception of increasing your social contacts within this kingdom." She didn't bother to look at him, keeping her eyes on what was being served to her. "The Duke and Duchess of Welby are very powerful Elites. They can do much to advance your cause. Whatever that may be."

"Good enough." He sat down and they shared a meal in complete silence as was becoming their routine. Together but miles apart.

CHAPTER FORTY-TWO

The morning of the picnic welcomed a glorious autumn day. The sky was a brilliant blue without a single cloud to obstruct its beauty.

Analisa had risen long before the sun and had requested an early meal in her sitting room. She was looking forward to a joyous day with her daughter and her friends and she was not going to allow an encounter with Thomas to ruin her mood. She would see him soon enough when they rode together to Palacio DiSanto.

The doctor had confirmed Evelyn's condition, and they were excited about sharing their happy news with everyone during the picnic this afternoon.

A knock on the door startled her. Goodness. She didn't realize she was wound up quite so tightly.

"Enter." She expected a maid coming to see to her comfort.

"Please forgive my rude intrusion, my lady. I need to speak with you, and it cannot wait." Marissa Jonas stood at the door with a serious look. Unsure if she was doing what was in her best interest. This could, at a very minimum, cause her to lose her position at Miramarea Abbey and quite possibly land her sacked without a reference, but she had to take the risk. It was the right thing to do.

"Good morning, Marissa. I do not believe anything could hamper my good mood this morning. Please come in."

Marissa entered, closing the door behind her. She walked to the center of the room with her hands folded at her waist. "I am afraid what I have to say will do nothing to brighten your day, my lady. And for that, I am sorry."

"You look absolutely pale, my dear." Analisa stood and went to help the young maid to the nearest chair. "Come, sit here and we will talk." Analisa took her chair and faced the young woman with motherly affection. "Now then. What tragic event has you in such a state?"

Marissa hesitated for a moment but soldiered ahead. "My lady, I must tell you that I am here under nefarious circumstances."

"How so?" Analisa was doing all she could to make the girl feel at ease.

"I was sent here to spy and to undermine you, my lady."

"That sounds ominous. Please continue. Who sent you?"

Marissa tried to gauge her employer's mood and possible reaction to the news. She liked this woman. Analisa had been nothing but gracious and caring for the very brief time Marissa had been in her home. "I am sorry to say, my lady. It was the Marchioness of Walsenburg."

Her daughter-in-law? But why? Ana had been under the impression their relationship was improving. They'd discussed the baby and her parents. Joseline had even volunteered to help at today's picnic. This made no sense.

Analisa schooled her reactions as she was accustomed to doing. She stared into nothing. She had never interfered in George's life. Prior to their marriage, she had tried to advise her son not to marry, but that had nothing to do with Joseline or her parents. It was the mere fact that George was much too young. He had never embraced the concept of sowing his wild oats. She simply wanted him to experience some of life before he settled down to home, hearth, and responsibilities.

Since their marriage, she had been nothing but supportive or so she thought. What would motivate Joseline to betray her in such a manner?

First things first. She needed the facts.

Sitting up, she addressed Marissa, who was obviously very shaken. Tears stained her cheeks and a look of panic clouded her eyes.

"Now, now. Let us take this one careful step at a time. You are clearly not completely to blame for the situation you find yourself in. If you had entered this bargain with malicious intent, you would not have approached me this morning with what could lead to your personal ruination."

She walked to the sideboard and poured the girl a glass of water. "Here, drink this slowly and we will begin at the very beginning."

Marissa began with her involuntary journey to the capital city, searching for her younger sister taken by her mother's reprobate of a brother for God only knows what. She never asked. Fortunately, she found her sister before anything untoward could happen to her and turned her uncle over to the authorities.

Unable to afford a passage home, she did what she could to keep them both alive. Once she had earned enough, instead of returning home, she brought her mother to the city to stay with them. Three mouths to feed on a housemaid's income was not easy.

Her position at Miramarea Abbey came purely by accident. The maid who was to fill the position fell ill and asked Marissa to step in for her. In hindsight, it is more likely the woman she substituted found out the kind of people the marquess and marchioness were and decided not to accept the position. Smart girl.

Analisa listened intently. She felt nothing but pity and sympathy for the young girl. "And now here you are. A housemaid and a spy and not being compensated adequately for the dual role." She hoped her attempt at humor would help to relax the young girl.

"I hope I do a much better job as a maid than a spy, my lady. I am happy to say the latter was not at all to my taste."

Both women laughed, uncertain of what to do next. If Ana had any trust in Thomas, she would have gone to him for help. Unfortunately, that was not an option open to her.

"So, tell me exactly what the marchioness expected you to accomplish while you were here."

"There was not much detail, my lady. I was to perform malicious little things such as ruin a meal while you entertained or loosen the seams on your gowns. I believe her goal was to embarrass you and ruin your reputation. I do not imagine her intent was to cause you physical harm."

"How are you communicating with her?"

"Each Tuesday and Thursday, she was to send a footman to Serenity Hall for an update. Anything I could tell her regarding your social calendar or personal goings on with the hall. That about covers it, my lady."

"Have you reported anything back to her thus far?"

"Nothing, my lady. Our first communication was to take place this coming Tuesday." She looked at Analisa for a moment. "I was supposed to sabotage today's picnic by adding this to the refreshments." She removed a small glass bottle containing a dark brown liquid from her apron. "I do not know what it is, but I was assured it would not cause any serious harm but…I just could not bring myself to go through with it." The tears returned. "I know I will lose everything, but I just could not live with myself if any harm came to you or to anyone at my hands."

"I will not allow any harm to come to you at my hands either, Marissa." Ana stood, walking calmly over to the window before she spoke again. "Keep going about your business as if nothing has happened. I will take care of everything. I can assure you that you will not be dismissed. In fact, I appreciate your honesty. It takes a great deal of courage to take the step you took today."

Marissa stood and curtsied. "Thank you, my lady. I do not know how to express my appreciation for your understanding and kindness."

"Keep this between us and I will consider it thanks enough. Now go on with you."

Alone once again, Analisa stood at the window for what seemed like hours. There were no words to express how devastated she felt at her daughter-in-law's treachery. But enough was enough.

CHAPTER FORTY-THREE

Everyone who was anyone had received an invitation to the Palacio DiSanto picnic. The grounds overflowed with visitors. The east lawns were manicured and evenly leveled for the comfort of the many guests.

A few tables had been strategically placed throughout the fields for the more mature patrons amongst them. For those unwilling or unable to enjoy a simple blanket on the grass to lay upon.

The west lawns were reserved for outdoor games with the clearing adjacent to the river designated for target shooting and archery.

The event was scheduled to commence at eleven that morning. Guests began to arrive at ten. Not many, but enough that the duchess decided to unofficially open the picnic early.

It was now half past one in the afternoon and the grounds were teaming with happy callers enjoying the sun, the food, and an abundance of friends.

The politicians as well as the matchmakers were out in full force making deals and executing plans.

The duke felt confident he had secured the support he required in parliament, thanks in large part, to the Baron and Baroness of Pennington.

Both Thomas and Analisa had explained at length the benefits to be had by both kingdoms when trade restrictions were eased. Day and seasonal laborers would have an easier time of crossing the border in either direction finding temporary employment without the burdens and delays caused when applying for temporary transient authorization from the kingdoms' offices of migratory affairs.

Sheep and cattle farmers in Sonastare could have wool and meat processed and prepared in Artemisia and distributed in both kingdoms. Corn and wheat growers in Artemisia would not need to construct mills when mills were abundant in Sonastare.

The Pennington Barony's advocacy was what made all the difference. If one Artemisian noble was willing to support the initiative, others would follow.

Analisa was still upset over this morning's developments but she managed to mask her feelings. There would be time enough later for the tragedies of life.

"Well done my dear. William feels his bills will all pass with overwhelming support thanks to you." Begrudgingly, she knew Thomas deserved much of the credit, but she was not prepared to offer him any recognition. Not yet.

"Then we can declare this picnic a monumental success."

"Done." Ada looped her arm around Ana's and began leading her toward the manor.

"Am I being dismissed?" She put on the most pathetic face she could manage. "Please do not dismiss me madam. I beg of you. I have twelve mouths to feed and my cat is gravely ill."

Ada slapped her on the arm as they walked. "That is simply not possible. You have an aversion to cats."

They entered the manor from one of the private side entrances designated for family members alone. Ada guided her toward the open door at the end of the hall where Marie and Maggie were already waiting.

Tea was just being set when in walked a footman with a tray containing Sherry, Claret and a bottle of brandy.

"Ladies, you are welcome to tea but as for me, I am in need of something more robust." She took the bottle of brandy from the tray and poured herself a generous portion of the amber liquid. "Would anyone care to join me?"

Two hands immediately went up.

Ada poured four glasses of brandy and gave one to each.

"If I recall accurately, I did not raise my hand." Analisa absently accepted the glass.

"You are the subject of this intervention. You do not get a vote. Drink up."

"I realize you are all anxious to help me with the Thomas situation, but I have no more information today than I did yesterday."

"Something has happened between yesterday afternoon and this morning." Ada took a seat next to Marie.

"We have all noticed the change in you my dear. We are your nearest and dearest. If we cannot help. We will find someone who can." Maggie waited patiently.

"Was it Thomas? Has he made more threats? Has he raised his hand to you?" Ada stood ready for battle.

"Very well. I will tell you. It has nothing to do with Thomas this time I swear it." She stood and began pacing without realizing it. "It is quite silly really." Three pairs of eyes stared in anticipation.

"This morning I discovered that an infiltrator was sent into my home disguised as a staff member to spy on me."

"Are you sure it was not Thomas? I would put nothing past that man." Ada was like a dog with a bone. It could start raining buckets ruining the picnic and somehow it would be Thomas' fault.

"I have reliable confirmation it was not Thomas." She walked over to the window and looked out over the east gardens where many were still relaxing on blankets eating berries. Not a worry or a care. God, how she envied them at this moment.

"They were sent in to relay private information and to cause havoc.

I am convinced the goal was not to cause permanent or lethal harm, simply to cause upset."

"Joseline." All three ladies seem to come to the same conclusion all at once.

Ana snapped her head in their direction. "How do you know that?"

"Sit, sit, sit." Marie urged her back. "We believe the marchioness is jealous of you and that this jealousy has escalated in the past few weeks since your return from the brink of death."

"Oh, do not be so melodramatic Marie. The brink of death? Really." Ada refilled her glass and brought the bottle to a table making it convenient to them all.

"The girl is a snobbish little shrew. She convinced herself she could be twice the marchioness you once were and is frustrated she cannot even get her servants to like her.

"You make a friend of every stranger while she is barely tolerated by her own family." They all looked at Ada as if she failed to share an important secret. "That is a story for another day."

"What sent her over the edge, was the crown giving you special permission to take up residence at Serenity Hall." Maggie had picked up the conversation from there. "When you married Mr. Smyth…"

"She did not marry Mr. Smyth." Ada interrupted.

"As far as the world is concerned, she did. Do we have any evidence to the contrary?" Maggie looked at Ada for a contradiction. When none was forthcoming, she continued. "That is what I thought." She turned back to face Ana.

"When you returned a married woman without a title, she made two huge but erroneous assumptions. First that you would be evicted from Bellstrand case in hand. That did not happen. You took up residence at a much larger estate leaving with a grace and dignity she has never possessed.

"Her second assumption was believing Serenity Hall was the dowager house belonging to the marquisate."

"She has been anticipating establishing her parents at Serenity Hall since she married George, one would assume." Marie joined in. "They still hold the title but cannot enjoy the benefits of the rank without funds. Residing at Serenity Hall on Bellstrand would give them the social foothold she imagined they would need to reenter society."

"But without capital they could not afford to live on Bellstrand. Who would support them for this long-anticipated reentry?" Analisa had nothing against the Duke and Duchess of Dials but had never given them or their situation much thought.

Again, all three responded in unison. "George!"

Ana looked at each of them individually then laughed. "That is ridiculous. George can barely support himself. If it were not for my occasional assistance, the marquisate would be in a greater state of devastation than the Dial Duchy."

"You know that, and we know that but apparently the marchioness does not have a clue." The two brandies were already working their magic on the duchess. "Moreover, the Duke and Duchess of Dials have no plans to reenter society in any grand manner. They are good people as are you and Darston. Your offspring however leave much to be desired."

Ada realized what she had said immediately and wanted to take it all back. "Oh dearest, please forgive me. I am not use to spirits and I forgot myself." She looked genuinely ashamed. "Marie is absolutely correct. I have a great big mouth and no filter."

"I never said that." She looked at Ana. "I have thought that on many occasions, but I have never actually said it out loud."

They all laughed.

"There is nothing to be forgiven my dear. You are my dearest friends. My sisters. If I cannot be honest with myself, I will be honest with you." It was time she took the blinders off. Past time. "George has always believed being a marquess was simply putting on the signet ring and lording over the world. His father and I did our best to teach him that with privilege and status come responsibilities and obligations. He never understood. I do not believe he ever actually cared to understand.

"For the past two years, I have hoped for an awakening but all I have experienced is utter disappointment. He is a married man with a child on the way. I cannot, I will not continue to prop him up.

"But how will I do that? He is my son. I cannot simply let him fail and let the marquisate go to ruin. What do I do?"

"You know what I will say my dear so I will refrain from saying it. I have hurt you enough this day. But I will ask you this. Leave the marchioness to us. You have enough to deal with." Ada looked like a child with a new game she could not wait to play.

Exhausted, she relented. "Very well. But remember she carries my grandchild and possibly the next Marquess of Walsenburg."

Ada looked insulted. "My darling. We do not deal in physical pain. We are genteel ladies. We deal in a much greater, longer lasting, and enduring agony. Social ruin. Leave it all to us."

Ana took a few extra minutes after her friends had returned to the picnic to pull herself together. The strains of the day, of the month, had taken their toll. As much as it pained her, she could no longer take responsibility for George's successes or failures. Joseline's maliciousness had severed any remaining feelings she had had for the girl.

Thomas had hijacked her life and she had a barony to uphold. Enough.

She walked out of the sitting room head held high. Decisions made, now all she had to do was find the strength to execute them. And then she saw him standing at the end of the long hallway with the enormous French doors as a backdrop. At first, she thought she was imagining him. But he began to walk toward her. He looked leaner, taller. His hair was long, barely grazing his shoulders. And then there were his eyes. She had always found peace in those eyes. Peace, strength, compassion, understanding and love. Yes, there was love in his eyes. Why had she not recognized it before?

"Good day, my lady. I have only just returned and was told…" He only stared at her. He took a step back. "I was just told the happy news. May I congratulate you on your marriage. I hope the baron knows how fortunate he truly is."

That was all it took. The flood gates burst open and she crumbled into him. He caught her as she knew he would. He had always been there to catch her.

Wrapping her arms around him with reckless abandon she began to cry.

CHAPTER FORTY-FOUR

Ryan DelCroft stepped off *The Emerald Princess* after nearly two months abroad. His adventure had been a great success, having uncovered and tentatively validated much of the treasure excavated in South Africa. Of course, the South African dig was a very small part of his impressive escapade.

He had not yet cataloged the inventory but had made a great start. There were several ships on their way to various ports in Europe with one making its way to Sonastare.

As exciting as it all was, all he wanted was to see Ana. He had written her a few letters, but considering the remoteness of his location, there was no guarantee she had received any of them.

Hiring a coach, he made his way home, where he unpacked, took a hot bath and a short nap before making his way to Bellstrand. Dressed in clean, modern attire for the first time in months, he made a quick stop at the tavern on the corner for something to eat.

Reaching the island ferries, he boarded *The Starling* and relaxed for the short journey that would deposit him by her side.

"May I get you anything, sir?" A young footman approached.

"Nothing for me, thank you." He looked around, finding an almost empty ship. "Is everyone on holiday? I seem to have *The Starling* all to myself this afternoon."

"Not at all, sir. The Duchess of Welby is hosting a picnic at Palacio DiSanto. Everyone is there now."

"Then it seems as if I have returned on the perfect day to celebrate. Tell me, what other important events have I missed while away?"

"All of the excitement this season has surrounded one of Bellstrand's most illustrious residents. Now the Baroness Pennington."

"We have a new baroness? That is exciting news. Are she and the baron in residence on the island?"

"They have just returned to the island for a few weeks as I understand it, sir. They are residing at Serenity Hall."

"Serenity Hall? Wonderful. The dowager Marchioness of Walsenburg must be hosting them."

"Oh no, sir. The former dowager marchioness is now Baroness Pennington."

Good Lord! I have been away for longer than I imagined. But he must have misunderstood. "Am I to understand she is also recently married?"

"Yes, sir. In late September if I am not mistaken." Someone was beckoning to him. "If you will excuse me, sir."

Ryan felt lightheaded for a moment. Ana? Married? A baroness? He took the opportunity of visiting with several of the passengers on board. Everyone confirmed the news.

Once on the island, he easily found transportation to Palacio DiSanto.

He found the estate teeming with people. Looking around, he was unable to locate Ana in the crowds. By the shooting range he found Thomas Smyth and Malcolm Gillam queueing up to take their turn.

"Good afternoon, gentlemen. Can either of you point me toward the Baron and Baroness of Pennington?"

Thomas smiled. "Locating the baron is extremely easy. You are speaking with him."

Ryan was taken aback. "I beg your pardon?"

Malcolm placed his hand on Ryan's shoulder. "Thomas here is the Baron Pennington. He and Lady Pennington married and recently assumed the Artemisian title."

Ryan could not move. All he could do was stare at Thomas. It took him a moment to regain his bearings. "Please forgive me, my lord. This is all quite a surprise. May I wish you every happiness in the world."

"Thank you, Mr. DelCroft. Now, if you are looking for the baroness, you may want to look inside the manor. I thought I saw her enter through the side entrance with Her Grace about an hour ago."

"Thank you, my lord. Once again. My congratulations." He bowed and headed toward the house.

Several friends and acquaintances crossed his path, but he didn't see any of them. It was as if he were walking in a haze.

He reached the manor, entering through the same door where the baron had seen Ana last. The hall was deserted, and all the doors closed. He could hear no sounds and assumed they had either entered the main house or had returned to the picnic.

And then, the door at the end of the hall opened. She stood there motionless for a moment. Something drove him forward. He wasn't certain if it was his feet moving him or some invisible force driving him towards her, but he was approaching her. *What will I say? What should I say?*

"Good day, my lady. I have only just returned and was told…" He was too close to her. He took a step back. "I was just told the happy news. May I congratulate you on your marriage. I hope the baron knows how fortunate he truly is." And suddenly, she was in his arms.

Ryan carried her back into the room from where she had emerged. With the door closed, they were Ryan and Ana again.

He laid her down on the fainting couch by the window and went to fetch her a glass of water from the tea tray.

Bringing it back to her, he found her with her face buried in the pillows, sobbing uncontrollably.

"Ana, please, tell me what is wrong." He made her take a few sips of the cool water. "Please, what has happened to get you in this horrible state?"

She was inconsolable. All she felt was pain and loss. So much loss.

He did not think, he felt, and he acted. He drew her into his arms and held her, giving her as much of his strength as he could. Whatever it was that hurt her, he would make it right.

She couldn't speak so he rocked her in his arms. Waiting patiently for the tears to subside.

Ana began to calm. She took a few more sips of water and sat up straight in an attempt to settle her nerves.

"Oh Ryan. I am so very sorry for that disgraceful display. I took one look at you and became an absolute watering pot." She made a weak attempt to straighten his jacket. "I have ruined your shirt with all my tears. You must think very poorly of me indeed."

An then it just happened. The words were just there. No hesitation, no regrets if he were cursed for it.

"You listen to me. You are the strongest most perfect person I have been blessed to know. My day, my life, begins and ends with thoughts only of you. I have loved you since the day we met, and I love you still, unworthy as I am.

"I do not know why God or Fate has allowed me to love you when I can never have you, but I will no longer deny what I feel for you.

"Now tell me what or who has hurt you and I will make them pay."

He felt twenty stones lighter. He also felt very foolish confessing his undying love to a married woman and one so far above his station. But the truth was that she would not chastise him for his declaration. She would likely tell him he was her good friend and that she cared for him as a sister would. It was irrelevant. Married or single, she was a temptation in which he could never indulge.

As it was, she didn't say a word. She reached for his face and, bringing it to her lips, kissed him. Deeply, passionately, thoroughly she…KISSED HIM!

As with the confession, his body took control of his mind. He enveloped her in his arms and deepened the kiss. Nearly thirty years of unconfessed love flowed between them. And continued to flow for the next twenty minutes. He could not get close enough to her to satisfy his needs.

A commotion outside in the corridor broke their spell. They separated, doing their best to right themselves, knowing they would be interrupted at any moment.

The door suddenly opened. "Ana, you must come quickly. Thomas has been shot."

Ada walked into the room and could immediately deduce what had happened only moments before she entered.

Ana jumped to her feet and joined Ada at the door. "Is he all right?"

"We are not certain. He fell back into the river when he was shot and was washed downstream. The men are all racing downriver in hopes of reaching him before he collides with the coral reef."

She looked back at Ryan. Not a word was uttered but he heard her all too clearly. Standing, he straightened his jacket and joined them by the door. "Of course I will come with you."

They all raced down the hall and into the yard, joining the crowd all heading for the river.

Ada was keeping up with Ryan just behind Ana. "It is about time you found the backbone to tell her how you felt."

He gave her a sidelong look. But said nothing.

CHAPTER FORTY-FIVE

"Send four men downriver to just before the reef. There is a narrowing of the waterway. If his body is still moving, it must go through that point before continuing." William was frantically giving instructions to noble and commoner alike. "Have a makeshift sickroom arranged in the green room. The doctor will need bandages and plenty of hot water. Mrs. Timmons will know what is necessary. Has the doctor been sent for?"

"Yes, Your Grace. He should be at the manor any moment. He will be instructed to wait until he meets with you." The young footman had just been sent to update William on the situation and to see to everyone's needs.

Although the water level was low at this time of year, the river was a powerful force. There were men crawling all over both sides. Some were tasked to construct barricades and catch nets. Others were responsible for keeping their eyes open for a body.

"If anyone sees anything, you are to fire a single shot into the air." He could only be clearly heard by the few who surrounded him, but he knew the message would be relayed quickly up and down the line.

Thomas's coat was rescued in tatters. It was bloody but not enough to assume massive blood loss. Not yet.

The desperate search continued into the night with nothing more found with the exception of the weapon Thomas was using, located not more than fifty feet from where he entered the water.

By midnight most had lost hope of finding him alive. The noblemen had sent their families home to await news and to keep the area and resources available for rescue efforts. It was time most of them retired and left what they now considered a recovery effort to William and his staff.

Analisa remained sequestered and surrounded by Evelyn, Ada, Maggie, and Marie, who never left her side. William feared an attempt against the baroness. He wanted to keep her close and safe.

Ryan was also part of the rescue and recovery teams but made frequent visits to see how Ana was holding up.

Those in close proximity to Thomas when he was shot were also requested to stay to be questioned by Collinsworth.

At just past one o'clock in the morning, William entered the green room followed closely by Collinsworth and two of his top lieutenants.

The duchess along with Ana and the other ladies all stood as they entered. Evelyn stayed by her mother's side while Archie joined the search. George had taken Joseline home, claiming she wasn't feeling well and needed some rest.

"Has he been found?" Ana was concerned but mostly confused. She did not have any real feelings for Thomas. He was, after all, her tormentor. Regardless, he was someone she knew and she was concerned for him as a person. Then there were the additional concerns for herself and her family and friends. Was this an attack against Thomas personally or was it a strike against the barony? Had he been shot because of her? Was she the intended target?

"No sign of him yet." William poured himself a brandy, offering the same to Collinsworth. The police chief declined. He needed his wits about him until the baron was found.

William emptied his glass and took a seat in the improvised circle of chairs in the middle of the room. "What do we know so far?"

"From what we have gathered, it was an accident. Witnesses believe a loaded pistol must have fallen from the weapon's table. We assume it went off when it made contact with the ground. Lord Pennington was in the queue awaiting his turn when he was struck and thrown into the river."

"How did the pistol fall? I specifically instructed our gunsmith to keep the weapons closely guarded at all times." William was taking the situation very personally.

"A croquet ball apparently hit the table by accident, taking everyone by surprise."

"Who launched the ball into the weapon's table?"

"Lady Arnell, Your Grace. Her eyesight is not what it used to be, and she lost her bearings."

Lady Arnell was in her mid-seventies, a lifelong resident of the island and above reproach.

"Can we release the witnesses to claim their beds? It is rather late."

"I have already done so, Your Grace. I did not think you would object."

William turned his attention on Ana. "I would recommend you stay with us for the time being. I am still not convinced there is not a threat hanging over your head. Until we know more, I must insist you remain under my protection."

"Arrangements have already been made, my love." Ada was not about to let Ana out of her sight under any circumstances.

CHAPTER FORTY-SIX

"Lord Trenton to see you, my lord." Dobbs bowed as Archie hurried past him in the doorway and into George's study.

"That will be all, Dobbs."

Only when the door was securely closed did they feel comfortable enough to speak.

"Any news on recovering Pennington's body?" Archie had stopped by Palacio DiSanto earlier that morning for an update. There was nothing to report.

"Our spies can neither confirm nor deny anything. Other than his coat, the baron has simply vanished." Being an overly cautious man, George did not want to make any assumptions. But he was feeling inexplicably confident their efforts were successful.

"I am not surprised. He was probably cut to pieces and pulled under by the currents of the reefs. Have we not had multiple reports of livestock accidentally falling into the river never to be seen again?" Archie was pacing nervously, unconsciously wringing his hands as he did so.

"It is possible. It is also possible he was rescued from certain death and is in hiding looking for his assailants." George was teasing him, but he felt great. With Thomas dead, his worries were over.

He had already concocted a plan to con his mother out of a hefty sum. He would convince her that with a possible heir on the way, George was turning over a new leaf. He would begin by establishing a diverse portfolio in his son's name. He would commit to making routine contributions to the account based on the recommendations of his investment team. The portfolio was to be exclusively in his son's name and could not be accessed until the heir had reached his majority. Being a loving mother and soon-to-be grandmother, he knew Ana would enthusiastically volunteer to contribute to the trust.

Of course, there was no portfolio per se. The funds would be funneled directly into George's personal accounts. No one but George and his mother would know of this fictitious trust, and by the time it was scheduled to mature, she would surely be dead. Or not. He really didn't care.

"Will you relax, Archie. Whether the body is recovered or not is academic. The search will go on for a little while longer. Once they accept the fact that the baron is dead, he will be declared so. My mother will, once again, have sole control of her finances and I will resume my unencumbered influence over her." Archie did not look convinced. George could not care less. Everything was working out his way for a change. "Now, what are we doing about Tenison?"

"He is adamant about gaining control over the Gables acreage. I have offered him the sixty thousand, but he is dead set on the land."

"Then he will simply have to wait. The issue is tied up in parliament. Until they settle the matter, the property remains mine."

"We both know he will not be content to simply wait for a resolution."

"What else can he do? He is welcome to approach the crown if he chooses. It is out of our control."

Archie genuinely feared Tenison. "I do not know, George. He can threaten to expose us."

"Then he loses the land, does he not? He will not risk it. Relax."

CHAPTER FORTY-SEVEN

It had been almost two weeks since the incident at Palacio DiSanto. Ana had returned to Serenity Hall with her daughter and her friends by her side.

The incident had been deemed a tragic accident, and life was slowly returning to normal.

Ryan was a daily visitor at Serenity Hall. His and Ana's relationship had been deepening, although they continued to keep their distance in public. It was impossible to hide it from her closest friends, who knew and encouraged the romance.

As much as he loved her, he knew there was no future in the cards for them. Her blood was too blue, too pure. His was mostly mud. But if he could not have her forever, he'd be satisfied to share what time he could with her.

"What are your plans, Ana?" Over coffee one late morning Ryan made an effort to look forward for them both.

"Honestly, I am uncertain. We have many things to address here in Salassio before we return to Dunnfee Court and address the Artemisian matters."

"What of your children? Evelyn is due in a few months and Joseline even sooner than that. Will you wait to see your grandchildren before your return south?"

"It will depend on several things. William tells me there must be an official declaration by the crown that Thomas Smyth, Baron Pennington is dead. Since his body was not recovered, a declaration is required before I can be proclaimed a widow. Once that is accomplished, as a widow, I will have the right and authority of controlling my own fate and finances once again. Until I marry, that is." She looked at Ryan with a sparkle in her eyes. He gave no sign of understanding. Or at least pretended not to.

"With the Sonastarian declaration, I will return to Artemisia and go through the process all over again. Pennington is an Artemisian title and will need to be approved by the Artemisian courts.

"I do not know how long this whole process will take, so it is quite possible I will be present for the birth of Joseline's child and maybe Evelyn's baby as well."

By now, Ryan knew the full story behind Ana's abduction and artificial marriage. He was very angry at first, wishing he could bring Thomas back to life just so as to kill him again, only this time with his bare hands.

With Thomas's death, there was no need in sharing the story with the whole world. It would be better for everyone concerned if she simply took on a second mantle of widowhood and faded back into relative obscurity.

Ryan reached into his satchel, retrieving a velvet case. "I wanted to give you this." He handed the case to her.

When she opened it, her heart nearly stopped. Inside she found a solid gold choker adorned with an assortment of various sized brilliant rubies and diamonds woven with south sea pearls. It must be worth a small fortune. He should not have done this. She knew he could not afford something this extravagant.

"Ryan, I cannot accept this. Think of everything you can do for the price of this unique piece. It is not that I do not appreciate the gift. I am flattered beyond words. I simply will never be able to put it on without questioning how much you have sacrificed for me. Please." She closed the lid and attempted to return it to him.

"I have paid nothing, nor have I sacrificed anything for it. It was what I demanded as compensation for my participation in the recent dig. But lest you believe that something this ostentatious represents my affection for you," he took the box in one hand and reopened it, "remove the choker if you will." Beneath the elaborate arrangement was a simple opal pendant. Much smaller than his first gift to her those many years ago.

"I thought to make up for my first botched attempt." He smiled. "This one is real."

She was so overwhelmed, words failed her. She found her composure after a few tears were shed. "Would it hurt you terribly if I told you I would not trade my first opal for all the diamonds, rubies, and emeralds in the world?"

They were in desperate need of a change of subject.

"Did I tell you? George is taking a turn for the better." She seemed optimistic.

"How so?" Ryan did not share her positive outlook where her son was concerned.

"He is establishing a trust in his son's name. He recognizes he has not lived up to his responsibilities where the marquessate is concerned and he wants to do better by his offspring by setting up an irrevocable portfolio guaranteeing his son's future financial security if not the investment's profitable success. Is that not wonderful?"

"I hate to point out the obvious, my dear, but with what funds exactly is he establishing this generous security for his son? A son, I must point out, who does not yet exist."

"He assures me he has been putting funds aside for his heir for the past year. He is requesting both I and the Duke and Duchess of Dials make a contribution. We all know the Duchy of Dials is not in a position to make any kind of donation at this time, so I have volunteered to match my own contribution on their behalf."

Ryan looked skeptical.

"They are good people, Ryan. I can afford the gift and I do not want them placed in the difficult position of having to refuse the opportunity due to a lack of funds." She hesitated for a moment. "I have asked George to keep this between us."

Ryan did not look convinced. The fact was that he did not believe a word of it where George was concerned.

"Please do not be like that. I have made a decision to no longer enable George in his downward spiral, but this is different. It is for my grandson and the future Marquess of Walsenburg."

"I completely understand. However, my approval is neither relevant nor necessary. You are an intelligent woman and the author of your own fate. In my eyes, you can do no wrong."

"Translation, I am crazy for doing it, but you love me anyway?"

CHAPTER FORTY-EIGHT

It was hours after the fateful shot in an abandoned cabin somewhere on the island. "Good God, man! Are you digging for gold?" Thomas had asked the same question multiple times in the past ten minutes. The doctor was working to remove the bullet, but it was lodged much deeper than anticipated.

"As you have been told on several occasions if you recall," Teddy was doing his best to hold him down while the doctor probed for the elusive projectile, "he is looking for a tiny bit of metal embedded in your shoulder."

"Tiny?! Your brain and your rod are tiny, you mongrel..." Thomas gave a loud scream at that point.

"I will have you know, I am very well endowed. And will knock you out by hitting you over the head with my considerable rod if you do not hold still."

Minutes later the doctor extracted the bullet, sterilized the area, and sewed up the wound.

Thomas was given a few minutes to rest while the doctor was dismissed and the room was put to rights once again.

"Now will someone please explain to me what the HELL happened?"

Teddy looked incredibly pleased with himself. "We shot you. Have you not been paying attention?"

"Teddy, will you put your joy at my expense aside for a moment to help me understand the circumstances surrounding my current condition? Or I swear on everything that is holy…"

"All right, all right." Teddy pulled up a chair next to Thomas's sick bed. "The plan had to be altered when Chase received last-minute instructions from Lord Trenton's man that you were to be eliminated within the next two days or the contract was void and he would find someone else to carry out the plan.

"We devised a scheme to have your assassination take place during the picnic this afternoon. The marquess arranged for two of our men to pose as footmen with one assisting the gunsmith at the shooting range.

"We were not clear on how we would execute the plan, and then the perfect opportunity presented itself. We had spotted the old lady chasing that silly ball all around the yard with absolutely no clue as to where she was or in what direction to aim her hammer."

"It is called a mallet," Thomas corrected him.

"Is that really relevant right now?"

"Go on then."

"Our man was given one of the game balls and was told to be prepared for any opportunity. The old lady was whacking away as you were queued up to take your turn on the range. She hit the ball, and our man threw a similar ball, hitting the table and sending several pistols and rifles to the ground. That is when Chase shot you.

"We had stationed three men just below the riverbank to pull your body down and out of sight. However, being the considerate man that you are, you graciously dropped ass first into our laps. Thank you for that by the way."

"You could have killed me, you know."

"No such luck. Chase is an excellent marksman. He could have placed the bullet anywhere he chose. I made a few suggestions which he disregarded, ultimately deciding to shoot you in the left shoulder. Inflicting temporary pain but with the least amount of incapacitation for you. See how much we care?"

Thomas gave him a lethal smirk. "Where are we now?"

"Location wise, we are in a shack on Serenity Hall grounds. It has been abandoned for years, so we are safe here.

"Situation wise, you are presumed dead. They found your bloody coat downriver, but that is all. The baroness is staying with the Duke and Duchess of Welby for the time being. The duke is not convinced your murder was an accident. He believes it may have been an attack on the barony. We will do our best to lay those doubts to rest."

"What of the marquess and the count?"

"They are elated. With you out of the way, they see a clear path to the baroness's coffers. Do you believe they will attempt to squeeze her now?"

"They have little choice. If George is not infused with a substantial amount of capital within the week, he risks the world finding out all his dirty little secrets."

"So how do we protect our interests?"

"I have already taken care of that. With the exception of household expenses and pin money, Lady Pennington has no authority to access estate funds. Here or in Artemisia."

Nearly two weeks had passed, and Thomas was recovering nicely. He still had limited use of his shoulder, but no infection had set in.

Teddy had just returned from his reconnaissance mission with some food and drink.

"What news?" Thomas was anxious for the next step in the plan.

"The baroness is back at Serenity Hall. This artist fellow, Ryan

DelCroft, has taken quite an interest in her. He could pose a threat." Teddy looked to Thomas for a reaction. Thomas seemed to simply brush it off.

"The marquess has sold the baroness some cock and bull story about a trust for his unborn son. I have not seen any evidence of a trust being established, so I am assuming this is how he intends to funnel capital from her pockets to his. Will the barriers you set up hold out?"

"They will." With some difficulty he sat up and accepted the plate Teddy offered. "Is everything else we discussed in place?"

"All but Tenison's downfall. Are you sure you want him permanently eliminated?"

"I am sure."

CHAPTER FORTY-NINE

The mood was privately festive. To the world, Baroness Pennington had just lost her husband. To her family and friends, her oppressor was presumed dead, and her life would soon be hers once more. They had petitioned the courts for an official declaration of death and were awaiting a response.

The dinner party was a very private affair. The Duke and Duchess of Welby were present as were Viscount and Viscountess Cross and Baron and Baroness Kelt. Analisa's son and daughter along with their respective spouses were also in attendance.

Ryan DelCroft had also been invited, as his presence at Serenity Hall was now a staple. He was still a little uncomfortable relating to these nobles on anything other than a professional level. For years, he had purchased art on their behalf and had always been treated with respect by one and all. But he had never seen himself as an equal. Now here he was, sharing a meal and discussing private family matters as if his opinion was of any importance.

Joseline was being tolerated and she knew it. Marissa Jonas had not made contact since she had entered Analisa's employ. Every attempt she had made to contact the young maid had met with failure. The girl may have fled to avoid the consequences of failing her mistress. Good riddance.

"I want you all to know how happy I am to have you gathered around me here this evening." They were all having after-dinner drinks in the family room when Analisa thought she would take the opportunity to address the group.

"It has certainly been a stressful few days, and although we are not through it yet, I wanted all of you to know how much your support has meant to me."

"We do for family, my dear," Marie volunteered. "So, tell us your plans once your widowhood has been officially declared?"

"I am in no hurry to return to Artemisia. I will be staying on at Serenity Hall to see my grandchildren safely delivered into the world. We may be awaiting the heirs to two prominent titles." She squeezed Evelyn's hand as she sat next to her on the settee.

Pitts appeared at the door. "My lady, Viscount Abernathy wishes to speak with you. He says it is important. Shall I inform him you are not receiving guests?"

George and Archie suddenly became very pale. They looked at each other, expecting Analisa would reject the intrusion.

"Please bring him in, Pitts. It must be important for it to bring him here at this hour."

Pitts departed, returning a few moments later with the viscount in tow. "Viscount Abernathy, my lady."

Reardon Tenison strolled into the family room brimming with confidence. "Good evening, Your Grace, my lords and ladies. Please forgive the intrusion but what I have to say could not wait." He looked at George then at Archie and winked. "I did not imagine such a distinguished audience when I decided to call on you this evening, but it is just as well."

He walked over to the mantel, lifting the brandy carafe. Before he poured himself a drink, he heard the intake of air from several of the ladies and the undeniable shuffling of men's feet preparing to do battle. He stopped and turned. "Please pardon my rudeness." He looked directly at Analisa. "May I, my lady?"

"That is your second offense this evening, Lord Abernathy. I will not pardon a third."

Reardon poured himself the drink and faced the assemblage. They were clearly ready to have him thrown out by brutal force preferably. He didn't care. He was angrier than they were and would not be silenced.

"Then let us dispense with the pleasantries and get to the heart of the matter." He emptied his glass and set it back on the mantel a little harder than he intended. "Your son and son-in-law have cheated me. And I demand satisfaction."

"How dare you come into my mother's home with such lies and accusations? Have you no respect for what she is going through? She has recently lost her husband, sir. Leave her be. Remove yourself at once." George put on his most indignant façade. "Out with you I said, or I will have you removed by force if necessary."

Reardon smiled and ignored him. From the look on Count Trenton's face, he had probably wet himself. Reardon chose to keep his attention focused on the baroness.

"Months ago, your son borrowed twenty-five thousand from me to invest in a risky shipping venture. Things did not go as expected and the ships were delayed. He then borrowed an additional seventeen thousand in an attempt to ride out the delay until the ships arrived. They never did. The loan came due. He has failed to pay what is due."

Everyone was looking at George. Joseline felt ill. Archie backed away, hoping Reardon would keep from mentioning him again.

It was Ryan who stepped forward. "And just exactly what do you expect the baroness to do? Your business is with the marquess and the count if I heard correctly. Moreover, how can we believe any of this to be true. Your reputation is not above reproach, my lord."

"I do not know who you are sir, but I do know you are not of the Elite. You do not have leave to address me in this manner. I suggest you sit down and shut up."

Ryan took two steps toward Reardon only to be stopped by a strong hand on his shoulder.

The Duke of Welby gave his shoulders a pat and stepped around him. "But you do know who I am, do you not?"

Reardon shrank a little. He'd forgotten the amount of power contained in this room. He still felt he had the upper hand, but he didn't want to tempt the fates.

"My apologies, Your Grace." He turned back toward Analisa. "My demands are simple, my lady. The marquess has already signed over the Gables acreage to me. The crown has placed a lien on the property for unknown reasons. I want that lien lifted and ownership transferred to me immediately."

"And you are assuming I have authority or influence over the crown?" Analisa looked confused. "What exactly do you expect from me, my lord?"

"I do not know what authorities you do or do not have, my lady. You do seem to be living a charmed life of late. All I know is that if that property is not in my name by week's end, the world will know the full extent of your family's involvement in sponsoring illegal trade." Now for the coup de grâce. "Oh, did I forget to mention the ships were carrying stolen antiquities and slaves?"

"That is utterly ridiculous!" George was desperate for this nightmare to end. "Those ships are carrying wheat and spices. There is nothing illegal in trading spices."

"Just moments ago, you accused me of lying, my lord. Are you now admitting to the ships' existence?" Reardon laughed. "The fact is that I can prove every single one of my contentions. But it is inconsequential. Your family's reputations, both of them, will be destroyed with the public accusation." He looked to Archie with his last remark.

"Now do I have your attention?"

"You certainly have mine." At the open doors to the rear of the room allowing access to the formal courtyards stood Thomas Smyth, Baron Pennington.

Everyone was caught by surprise and seemed frozen in time and space.

Reardon was the first to regain his composure. "Still alive, I see. Do not interfere in matters that do not concern you, Baron. This is much above your station."

As if on cue, from behind Thomas six rather impressive-looking men entered the room, the smallest of whom was well over six feet tall and built like a bull. Thomas addressed the man immediately to his right. "Would you be so kind as to have Viscount Abernathy removed from the premises."

"You would not dare…"

"No need to be gentle about it," he instructed casually without taking his eyes off Reardon.

"Broken bones?" Teddy asked humorously.

"If necessary."

Teddy gave the signal and two men flanked the viscount. They each took an arm and half dragged him from the room. "You will live to regret this. By morning the whole kingdom will know your dirty little secrets." His voice faded as he was dragged further and further away. He continued to threaten but he could no longer be heard.

Thomas walked up to Analisa, taking her hand in his and kissing her cheek. "Have you missed me, my love?"

Analisa quickly regained her composure. "I am grateful you are unharmed, my lord."

"I would not go that far. I was shot."

"Where have you been all this time?"

"Recuperating, my dear. I feared for my life and continued safety, so I elected to remain in hiding until I was certain the danger had passed." He looked around the room. "I see the prospect of my death did not cause you too much worry. I am so grateful." He turned toward everyone in the room. "So grateful to you all for all the support you have showered on my devoted wife during these trying times."

"Perhaps it would be better if we were to discuss this in private, my lord." Analisa looked to her family. No one seemed to be making any effort to depart.

"I do not think that a good idea, Ana." Ada was staring daggers at Thomas.

"By all means. I welcome everyone to stay."

"Thomas, please. There is no need to patronize my family. What is, should remain between the two of us. Let us deal with the matter in private. I beg of you."

Thomas took the empty seat furthest away from the gathering but with the best vantage point. His shoulder was bothering him, and he needed to rest the limb.

"I will assume my wife has brought you all current on our arrangement." He looked at each face carefully. He could see all but her daughter had been made aware of the situation. "Good, then we can dispense with the pretenses."

"What do you want, Smyth? What is your objective in taking advantage of Lady Pennington? Did she wrong you in some manner? Have we?" Ryan had come to stand by Analisa's side. Their hands were almost touching but not quite.

"We will prove this all a hoax and then you will be made to pay. I promise you," Ernesto Grossman, Baron Kelt threatened.

"Not in time, my lord, I can assure you."

"In time for what, if I may be so bold?"

Thomas had to admit he had misjudged Ryan DelCroft. The man was angry and ready to do battle. Good for him.

"Why the dramatic return now, my lord?" Dwight Bellings, Viscount Cross questioned.

"Rumor has it, I am to be declared officially dead in the not too distant future. I could not let that happen. So, here I am. Returned

229

safely to home and hearth and to the bosom of my loving wife and partner. Is it not a lovely story?" He looked around. "Not a single tear. How disappointing."

He sat up straighter in his chair. "Now, let us get down to business. First of all, everything that slimy little rat shared with you is true and accurate. The marquess and the count are participating in the illegal trade of antiquities and slaves. The ships' documents and manifests will confirm this. Moreover, once their co-conspirators are rounded up and arrested, they will not hesitate to point the finger at these two reprobates in order to save their own skins."

"How dare you?!" George made a very weak attempt at indignancy.

"Do not push me, lad, or I will have you, too, removed by force. And do not think I will not do it."

Thomas made a second attempt to relax his aching shoulder and to readdress the entire gathering. "This is not their first shipment of such cargo. It is, in fact, their third and their largest haul to date. When news of this spreads, as it is bound to, your family's reputations will be ruined for certain."

"Enough! I repeat, what exactly is it that you want?" At some point Ryan had taken Ana's hand in his. He now stood directly in front of her as if to physically protect her from Thomas's attacks.

Thomas smiled. "Everything."

"Please elaborate." Ana felt strong and she felt protected.

"Your Artemisia inheritance is larger than you have been led to believe. I want you to sign over your inheritance to me."

"I give you my inheritance and you will grant me a divorce?"

"Simple as that. You still have your widow's pension and your parents' legacy in Sonastare. You keep the barony in Artemisia along with its entailed assets, but I get everything else."

"And you will disappear from my life permanently?"

"Never to be seen again." He looked her straight in the eye. "What do you say?"

"Done." Analisa felt an enormous sense of relief.

With the exception of Ryan, everyone objected at once. "Ana, you cannot give in to extortion."

"He is a villain and a scoundrel. You cannot let him win."

"We will not give up. We will continue to fight all the way to the crown if necessary."

Ana looked to Ryan. "What do you think?"

He was calm and in complete control of his emotions. "You will never miss what you did not know existed. It is cheap at twice the price to have this millstone removed from around your beautiful neck."

"What of us? What of your children? What of my son's inheritance? Will you leave him destitute? Are you really that selfish, Mother?"

The veil had been lifted. For the first time since his birth, Analisa saw her son for the selfish, self-centered, greedy little beast he really was. Suddenly, Thomas was no more than a nuisance. The real villain was the pathetic excuse for a man to whom she had given life.

Analisa released Ryan's hand and walked over to her son. "My dear boy." She brought her hands up to cradle his cheeks. "I love you and your sister with all of my heart. I have since the day you were each delivered into my arms.

"Your father and I went out of our way to show you both love and support since the day you were born. We had such high hopes for you as the next Marquess of Walsenburg. We believed you would bring the marquessate to new heights."

Her hands dropped and her eyes turned dark. "What a disappointment you have turned out to be. You have placed the family and the title in jeopardy to pad your pockets. You have never amounted to much and you never will. I do not say this out of a desire to hurt you. It is simply a fact of life. Take yourself and your wife and be gone from my sight."

She returned to Ryan's side, directing her next comment to her son-in-law. "Archibald Maddahs, eighth Count of Trenton. You have the responsibility of protecting and cherishing my daughter and the child she carries. You may still be able to salvage what is left of your reputation. I would recommend you do so with alacrity. Hurt my daughter in any way and you can be certain to count me among your enemies, for I will do everything in my power to remove you from their lives. You, too, are requested to leave my presence."

With George and Archie gone, Thomas addressed the group. "Now I would like for everyone to leave. I wish to discuss the details of the dissolution of our marriage with my dear wife in private."

"It is all right. I am confident Thomas means to do me no physical harm." Analisa addressed them all with a smile attempting to set all of their minds to rest. She volunteered to meet at Marie's home for tea the following day.

With a great many reservations and foot dragging, everyone departed. Everyone but Ryan.

"Your services are no longer required, Mr. DelCroft. If you will kindly vacate the premises?" Thomas had dismissed his men and was attempting to do the same with Ryan.

"You will have to kill me, sir." There was a determination and a commitment in his demeanor no one would have expected from a curator's son.

"I can do that." Thomas wanted to see how far this man would be pushed.

"You can try." He wrapped Ana protectively in his embrace. "Are we to spar all evening or do you have something else to say?"

"Is there something untoward going on between the two of you? Infidelity is a very serious offense and grounds for divorce. I could end up with much more than I was expecting. And you with much less."

"Only if the unfaithful party is a woman." Ana was not intimidated.

"You presume too much, sir. We all know there is no marriage here. Without a legal union the rules of infidelity do not apply."

"Ah, but can you prove we are not legally married?" Thomas

232

paused, letting it sink in. "For I can prove we are." This was fun but it was time to bring things to an end. "Mr. DelCroft, am I to understand you are in love with Analisa?"

"The question is presumptuous, sir." He stumbled a bit. "And irrelevant. I will stand by her side regardless."

"I see." He looked to Ana. "And do you, likewise, care for him?"

Ana looked at Ryan as if really seeing him for the first time. "Yes, I love him."

"Well then, my job here is done." He stepped around them to retrieve his hat and gloves. "My solicitor will be by to see you in the morning and iron out the details of the dissolution of our marriage."

Walking to the door he took one last look at Ryan and Ana. "This worked out much better than I had imagined." He then yelled into the hall, "Pitts! My horse if you please."

He was gone.

CHAPTER FIFTY

The following morning Ryan arrived early to break his fast with Ana. He did not want her to face Thomas's solicitor alone.

They had a light meal, neither of them being very hungry.

Ana had dispatched notes to all her friends and her daughter that all was well and that she would plan on seeing them at Marie's home at four that afternoon.

Sharply at ten, Pitts knocked on the morning room's door, announcing visitors. "They did not volunteer their names, my lady, but mentioned you would be expecting them."

"Yes of course, Pitts. Please show them into the study. We shall be down presently." She turned to Ryan. "Shall we?" She was dreading the meeting, knowing she was about to hand over much of what her parents had worked so hard for and intended for her. But she also knew this would rid her of Thomas Smyth permanently and she needed to take that step before she could take the next.

They walked together to the study where three gentlemen patiently waited.

"Good morning, my lady."

Analisa was taken completely by surprise. She had expected a savvy attorney or two, but this was something that had never crossed her mind. Maybe this was a simple coincidence and these gentlemen were here for different reasons.

"Your Grace, Mr. Granger. Has something happened?" A hundred horrible things crossed Analisa's mind. Bellmorrow had caught fire, the twin kingdoms had declared war, Dunnfee Court had been repossessed to satisfy back taxes.

"Nothing tragic has occurred, my lady." Aguste Arcady motioned her to join him around the study's enormous oak desk.

Analisa remembered herself. "Your Grace, may I present my dear friend, Mr. Ryan DelCroft."

Aguste gave him a slight nod.

"Ryan, I have the honor of presenting to you His Grace, Aguste Arcady, Prime Minister of Sonastare."

Ryan gave a formal bow. "I am honored, Your Grace."

She continued. "This is Mr. Miles Granger. Our man of business for the Barony of Pennington, and…" She did not recognize the third man present.

The prime minister did the honors. "Forgive me, my lady, this is a colleague; Alexander Brown."

"It is an honor and a pleasure to meet you, my lady." Alexander bowed.

She thought his voice sounded familiar. The manner in which he said "my lady" struck a chord.

"Mr. Brown." She acknowledged him as was appropriate.

"If we can get started, my lady?"

"Yes of course. To what do I owe the visit?"

"We are here representing Thomas Smyth's interests as well as your own."

It finally dawned on her. These were the attorneys Thomas had told them to expect. Who was Thomas Smyth and why was the kingdom's prime minister here representing him? And what did Miles Granger have to do with all of this?

"I have here a letter of annulment." He handed the document over to her. "This officially dissolves the union as if it had never existed. I will need your signature at the bottom."

"Annulment? I was under the impression we would be filing for a divorce."

"Circumstances being what they are, the annulment is more appropriate and much less complicated, I assure you."

Confused, Ana signed the instrument of annulment, handing it back to the prime minister.

The prime minister handed her a second document. "This is a certification of autonomy. It officially recognizes you as your own primary agent. No one with the exception of His Majesty from this day forward will have any power or influence over what is yours. Any challenges to this edict will face the king's justice.

"I believe that concludes our portion of today's business." Aguste stepped aside, allowing Miles to take the floor.

Ana felt that there were still questions to be answered. "At the risk of jeopardizing my own good fortune, Your Grace. What of the documents transferring my inheritance into Mr. Smyth's name?"

The prime minister and Alexander both smiled as Miles addressed her concerns. "There will be no transfer, my lady. Mr. Smyth was only interested in protecting you and the kingdom from threats he saw as coming too close to you and to the crown. If you will make yourself comfortable, my lady, I will go over everything in detail."

Ana and Ryan both sat in the chairs facing the great desk. From his satchel Miles withdrew several documents, stacked them neatly on the desk before him, and sat down.

"I would like to begin with an apology. You were purposefully kept in the dark regarding many details surrounding the barony. This was done for your protection as well as ours, my lady. I hope you can forgive us."

"What sort of details have been kept from me?"

"To begin with, your personal fortune far exceeds anything we have led you to believe. Ten years of solid investments and no withdrawals have netted you an inheritance well over six million in assets. You are officially the single wealthiest person in the twin kingdoms after the royal families.

"A full and detailed accounting of your portfolio will be made available to you in the coming weeks.

"Along with the title, you now enjoy a seat in Artemisia's house of nobles. You will not be the first or the only woman in Artemisia to hold office, but you will be the most powerful. We are confident you will use your power wisely."

"I am afraid I know very little regarding Artemisian politics. I would never forgive myself if I assumed a position only to cause more harm than good." Ana was suddenly overwhelmed with the responsibilities.

"I do not see this as a problem, my lady. Not with Mr. DelCroft by your side." Miles glanced at Ryan.

"You have my permission to speak freely, Mr. DelCroft." Aguste waved him on to speak.

"I am one of the kingdom's ambassadors abroad."

Ryan was looking at her for signs of anger or betrayal. She had had enough to deal with these past few months. The last thing she needed was to find out the man she loved had lied to her as well.

"I was recruited more than fifteen years ago by the privy council and trained as a negotiator for the kingdom. Most of my so-called archaeological expeditions were actually political missions for His Majesty." He reached out for her hands. "Were I at liberty to share this part of my life with you, I would not have hesitated. I hope you will not hold it against me."

"So, this archaeological dig in South Africa? A deception?"

"No, there was a genuine dig. With a little politics on the side." He smiled coyly.

She was smiling as tears rolled down her cheeks. "Good heavens! Ambassador DelCroft! It is an honor and a privilege, sir."

Without hesitation, Ryan reached out and kissed her in front of God and country. Not one person in the room batted an eye.

When they looked up, Miles and Aguste were both smiling. "May we continue?"

"Of course. Please go on, Mr. Granger."

"As baroness, you have the option of taking up the parliamentary seat yourself or of delegating a proxy to represent you. The representative must be approved by the Artemisian Parliament of course."

Ana looked at Ryan. "Would this require him to give up his position as ambassador?"

"Not at all. Particularly if he assumes the permanent position as Sonastarian Ambassador to Artemisia." Aguste had been expecting this request and had had it approved by the king himself prior to his arrival here today.

"And finally, all funds utilized by Mr. Smyth while in the role of baron have been returned to the barony coffers without exception. That is all the official news I have to share with you this day, my lady, unless you or Mr. DelCroft have any further questions?" Miles looked at Ana and at Ryan.

"This is all a great deal to digest, Mr. Granger. I am certain we will have a great many questions in the near future."

"And I will be here to address them at your own good pace, my lady."

"Now that we have taken care of all official matters, it was requested I return this to your care." Aguste handed her the barony's signet ring. Thomas had been wearing it the previous night.

Ana looked at Aguste with a little hesitation. "Was Mr. Smyth one of your men, Your Grace?"

"Not exactly, my dear, but we do work together from time to time."

Everyone stood. "We do have a few more matters to attend to and would like to request the use of your study for the remainder of the morning if that is acceptable." Aguste knew she would not refuse.

"Of course, Your Grace. Our home is yours for as long as you need it."

"I must warn you; my next few audiences will be difficult for us all and will have a direct impact on your loved ones. I give you my word that what we are about to do is inevitable and essential. However, we are hoping that our methods will effectively minimize the negative fallout for you and your family."

"Do you require our presence, Your Grace?"

"No, my lady. Simply your patience and your understanding."

"You have it, Your Grace."

Ana and Ryan were returning to the morning room when Pitts opened the main doors to George and Archie.

Rudely pushing Pitts aside, George marched up to Ana, ignoring Ryan completely. "What is the meaning of this, Mother? We received a summons to present ourselves at Serenity Hall this morning promptly at eleven. Do you have anything to do with this?"

"She does not!" An authoritarian and booming voice from the study door. "You will both join me in the study immediately."

George, of course, recognized the prime minister's voice. "Yes, Your Grace." He hurried to the study, where he and Archie both bowed to Auguste, who held them at attention for a moment before bidding them enter the library.

Auguste closed the door behind him. Only he, George, Archie, and Alexander remained.

"Take a seat, gentlemen."

George and Archie took the seats previously occupied by Ana and Ryan. The prime minister took the seat behind the desk while Alexander looked on from beside the fireplace.

"I assume you are aware why we are here today?"

"I...We...No, Your Grace. Is something wrong?" George was stuttering and Archie was about to soil himself. Again.

"Your ships have been located and seized by the crown. Those you sought to sell as slaves are en route to their points of origin as we speak. The antiquities have been confiscated and will be returned to their countries of origin once they have been authenticated and cataloged."

"But we had nothing to do with the shipment, Your Grace. It was Viscount Abernathy who is responsible for all of this. We are innocent, sir, I swear."

"That will be for the courts to decide but I must tell you, the evidence against you is overwhelming."

How? Who? What were they to do now? *Mother! She will...*

"Lord Walsenburg, Lord Trenton, although you will maintain your titles as a royal courtesy, you are both forthwith stripped of all rights and privileges associated with those titles.

"For the sake of your families and your future heirs, you will be allowed to continue living under the appearance of nobility. All entailed and unentailed properties and assets associated with your name and with the titles will be placed under the supervision of a court receiver. You are not allowed to make any decisions regarding the titles and will leave the upbringing of your heirs to royal discretion.

"Any efforts to violate or attempt to violate these conditions will be considered treason and punishable by death. Have I made myself sufficiently clear?"

"Yes, Your Grace." George could barely get the words out.

"Now get out of my sight, both of you, before I reconsider and recommend your hanging."

They both scrambled to their feet, fleeing the study and the manor.

Aguste looked to Alexander. "Has the Abernathy situation been addressed?"

"He was arrested this morning. The title has officially reverted back to the crown along with all assets, entailed and otherwise. Reardon Tenison is nothing more than a soon-to-be convicted criminal."

"Then our job here is done, would you not say?"

"I would indeed, Your Grace."

Ryan and Ana enjoyed a moment of peace and quiet after the morning's excitement.

"Ambassador DelCroft." Ana bounced the words around for the umpteenth time since their meeting with the prime minister. "It certainly has an official ring to it. I like it. And soon you will be the permanent and official ambassador to Artemisia and take up a seat on the Artemisian council."

"Yes, it has certainly been quite a day. What is next, a duchy of my own?"

"I cannot speak to a duchy, but what would you say to a barony?"

Ryan snapped his head to Ana, who was holding out the signet ring.

"Ambassador DelCroft. I realized it is a woman's place to wait for a proposal, but we have been wasting too much time as it is. So, I am taking the liberty of breaking with conventional traditions and asking, will you do me the honor of becoming my husband?"

"As a baroness and the wealthiest woman in the twin kingdoms, you do not need to break traditions, my darling. You set them." He went down on one knee in front of her and kissed her. "Of course I will marry you. Is this afternoon too long of an engagement period? It certainly is for me."

CHAPTER FIFTY-ONE

"Your Majesty, Their Royal Highnesses Prince Edward Alexander and Prince Christopher Grayson."

The queen was relaxing in her private quarters when Christopher and Edward arrived at the palace.

She put down her novel and rushed to greet her sons. "My darlings. It is so wonderful to see you both."

"Mother, you are radiant as ever." Edward picked his mother up and swung her around like a rag doll.

"Edward! Put me down. You know that is not proper behavior for a royal prince of Sonastare."

Once on the ground she approached her youngest. "Christopher? I am quite annoyed with you. I have been requesting your presence for nearly three months, and you have failed to make an appearance. What have you been up to?"

"Mother." Christopher kissed his mother on both cheeks. "I have not received a single summons from my sovereign queen. If I had I would have rushed to your side at once."

Queen Shahjalal slapped him on the arm. Christopher did his best to suppress the painful wince. "You impertinent boy. You may have me wrapped around your finger, but your father is a different matter. He wants to see you the moment you arrive."

"And just where may we find our sire at this moment?"

"I would assume with Prime Minister Arcady at this time of the morning. Off you go. He is a bear when kept waiting."

The king and prime minister were just finishing up when a palace guard announced his sons.

"Christopher. Where have you been for the past three months? You have had your mother worried to death. I was about to send out the royal guard to track you down."

"I was hiding in the mountains, planning the overthrow of the kingdom. Edward and I plan on having you and Mother committed and Horacio locked up in a monastery for safekeeping."

The king was still a bit distracted with recent developments in the kingdom. "Very good. Very good."

Christopher and Edward just looked at each other. "Is there something you require of me, Your Majesty?"

Christopher's words finally registered. Maximilien gave his youngest son a disapproving stare. "You do realize you speak treason?"

"Oh Father. You know I jest. Sonastare is much too small for me to bother with. If I were to truly plan a coup, it would be of England, Spain, or France."

The boy was incorrigible. "I am afraid we have had an upset in the kingdom. Reardon Tenison, the former Viscount Abernathy, has been found guilty of treason. Are you familiar with the man?"

"I cannot say that I am, Father. Does this present a problem?"

"Not at all but I do need the circumstances surrounding his conviction investigated. I would like for you to use your anonymity to uncover what you can. Can you do that for me, my boy?"

"Consider it done, Father. Will there be anything else?"

"No, you may go. Please keep Arcady and your brother informed. If swift action is required, I want for them to be prepared."

"As you wish, Your Majesty."

"Edward." The king now addressed his spare heir. "You are second in line to the throne. It is time you begin considering choosing a wife."

"As you wish, Your Majesty."

Both young men executed a perfect military about-face and exited the room.

Waiting for them was Prime Minister Arcady. "Your Highnesses." Aguste bowed low. "We have released our hold on the Gables acreage. The purchase has gone through. They are now the property of Baroness Pennington without conditions."

"The last piece has fallen into place." Christopher could not have been happier for her.

"Will you ever tell her who you really are?" Edward understood the need for secrecy, but he always regretted Christopher not receiving any credit for his contributions to the kingdom and its people.

"It is not my choice, Alex. Our parents have zealously protected our identities our entire lives for very good reasons. Until the time comes, His Royal Highness Prince Christopher Grayson Morejón must remain a mystery. But what of it? As long as Thomas Smyth is allowed to go out and play."

EPILOG

Dunnfee Court, Artemisia 1851

"**M**y lady. They have arrived." Powers was beaming with delight, knowing how happy the children's visits always made the baroness.

Both Joseline and Evelyn had given birth to boys four months apart.

Ana and Ryan made the journey to Salassio twice each year to spend time with the children. In the summer, both boys were sent south to Dunnfee Court, where they would spend most of the season with their grandmother and Uncle Lion as the boys had dubbed Ryan since they were old enough to speak. They had had difficulties pronouncing their "r," so Lion replaced Ryan. The baron could not be happier. They made a few weak attempts to correct their pronunciation, but Ryan wouldn't hear of it.

Shortly after their wedding, Ana received word that the crowns of both kingdoms had found it fit to once again make the Pennington Barony whole. This meant it held massive amounts of property on both banks of the Mara River and in both kingdoms. Everyone symbolically accepted it as if uniting two kingdoms in marriage. The impact was miraculous and unifying.

"Gammy!" Two young boys barely six came running into the room and propelled themselves into Analisa's open arms. These two were not opposed to showing massive amounts of affection anywhere and at any time. These were her boys. "Patic wants sweets."

Lord Patrick James Hastings was George's son and heir to the marquessate. His slightly younger cousin, Lord Liam Edward Maddahs, was Evelyn's, and heir apparent to Count Trenton.

As it turned out, the same royal receiver was assigned to both titles. George and Archie had bristled like caged animals for the first two years under the yoke of the crown's supervision. But they had eventually settled into their new roles as figureheads. They refused to participate in anything that involved Ryan. They felt Ana's new husband was beneath them both and unworthy of their attention.

This suited Analisa and Ryan perfectly. Little did both those idiots realize, the crown's appointed receiver reported directly to Ryan, who, together with Miles Granger, controlled their entire destiny. Both titles were prospering greatly but neither lord could take credit nor advantage of their mounting success.

"Gammy." Patrick hopped onto her lap. "Nanny says if I eat too many sweets, I will get too obse. What is obse?"

Before Ana could address the question, Liam responded. "Obese, not obse, Patic. Cook is obese. So is Tessa the mean maid at our house. Your mommy is obese. Isn't she, Gammy?"

Joseline had been putting on quite a bit of weight over the past few years. But that was understandable. She had been ostracized by every society matron on the island.

Ada along with Maggie and Marie had gradually but thoroughly managed to turn the entire Elite against her.

With the exception of Evelyn, who was, once again, expecting, George, Joseline, and Archie had become relative recluses. Ryan, via the receiver, made sure they doted on their children, but they were not allowed to make any decisions of consequence where the heirs were concerned. Again, unbeknownst to them, Ana had complete control on how the boys were raised.

There were, however, growing concerns regarding the subversive factions still operating in the twin kingdoms. In bringing Reardon Tenison to justice, they had opened a Pandora's box of troubles. Now it was up to Christopher and the crown to get to the bottom of things.

Liam snuggled next to Ana on the settee. With Patrick on her lap and Liam by her side, Ana was in heaven. "Gammy? Will you tell us a story about the Garrix wars?"

"Again? You have both heard those stories a hundred times each." What they didn't know was that she always added some new and exciting detail just to make them happy. Once, there was even a dragon.

"Pllleeeaaassse?" two little voices pleaded.

"Very well. If I must." She kissed each of them on the forehead.

"Once upon a time. A very long time ago…"

Lightning Source UK Ltd.
Milton Keynes UK
UKHW041918150621
385583UK00001B/74